LOOKING FOR GORDON
THE SHAPE OF LOVE

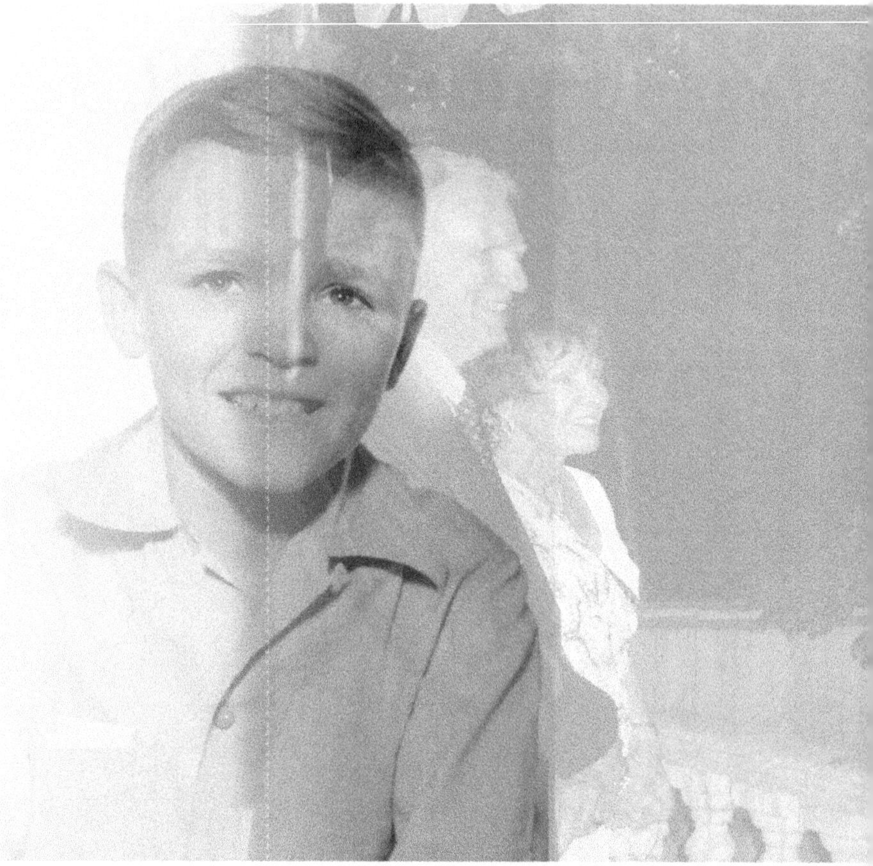

LOOKING FOR GORDON

THE SHAPE OF LOVE

CAROLYN TAYLOR-WATTS

PUBLISHED IN 2021 BY
KINETICS DESIGN, KDBOOKS.CA

Copyright © 2021 by Carolyn Taylor-Watts

All rights reserved. No part of this publication may be reproduced or transmitted in any form or by any means, electronic or mechanical, including photocopying, recording, or any information storage and retrieval system, without permission in writing from the publisher.

Published in 2021 by
Kinetics Design, KDbooks.ca
ISBN 978-1-988360-69-0 (paperback)
ISBN 978-1-988360-70-6 (ebook)

Cover and interior design, typesetting, online publishing, and printing by Daniel Crack, Kinetics Design, KDbooks.ca
www.linkedin.com/in/kdbooks/

Contact the author at
www.carolyntaylorwatts.com

In memory of my beloved husband, Gordon Watts,

who died on May 21, 2019

The Empty Door

I will meet you,

At the empty door,

Enter the atrium of dreams once bold,

Regrets untold,

Walk the corridor

Of restlessness,

Bathe in the pool

Of forgetfulness,

And in the grand salon,

Where the threads of life,

Now grey,

Fray in the dying light,

Share verses,

Forged by the night.

— Ian Thomas Shaw

Contents

Acknowledgements   10
Prelude   11

1   In the Beginning   13
2   The Man at the Other End of the Corridor   16
3   Are You Available?   19
4   Will You Marry Me?   21
5   We Are Us   24
6   Together   25
7   A Wedding   26
8   Who Are You?   30
9   The Pageant of My Universe   36
10   Patterns Interrupted   36
11   Beds We Sleep In   40
12   New Zealand   40
13   This Is Us   43
14   You Can Do Anything   46
15   A Literary Adventure   47
16   To See the World   49
17   A Side Trip to Hospital   50
18   Patras   54
19   A Bedtime Obsession   56
20   What Do We Owe the Dead?   57
21   The Empty Door   60
22   The Empty Chair   61
23   Everyone Inherits Something   62

24	Looking for You	65
25	The Peloponnese	68
26	New Zealand Again	70
27	A Southern Journey	74
28	Where Are You?	76
29	Another World Down Under	76
30	Us at Home	79
31	Christchurch	81
32	Portugal	84
33	Toronto Afterward	85
34	Istanbul	86
35	Cappadocia, Turkey	91
36	Spectral Images	94
37	In the Mountains of Central Turkey	113
38	Izmir	115
39	Flying Home	117
40	Love That Lasts a Million Years	117
41	We Were Us	120
42	Marriage, Grief	121
43	Florence	123
44	New York City	127
45	How Our Things Outlast Us	129
46	Learn Something New, Walk a Path from Yesterday	131
47	Berkeley Street and Family	135
48	Britain	136
49	A Nightingale Sings	140
50	London	143
51	Illness and Surgery	145
52	A Last Return to New Zealand	149

53	At Home	150
54	This Is What I've Made of My Life	152
55	A Prankster	155
56	What We Owe the Dead Once More	155
57	Early Images	157
58	A Professional Life	159
59	Young and Old Life	162
60	Afterward	163
61	Shadows Creeping	165
62	Shadows Gathering	166
63	Your Life: *Vita, Gloriosa Vita*	170
64	After	175
65	Is There Any Life After …?	176
66	This Is, and Was, Us: Our *Vita, Gloriosa Vita*	179
67	Newfoundland	182
68	Cobalt: Ashes to Ashes …	186
69	One of a Kind	191
70	Six Months Is an Eternity	193
71	Marriage	194
72	More Images	195
73	Christmas	197
74	Brothers	198
75	I Will Meet You at the Empty Door	200
76	Ellicottville	201
77	Mexico	202
78	A Year Is Nothing	203
79	What to Do with Love	206
80	Healing Is Remembering Well	208

Acknowledgements

Thank you to Paul Henderson for his reading of the various drafts of my story and his feedback. And thanks to Dvora Levinson for her always insightful comments and unwavering support. Thanks, too, to Michael Carroll for his fine editing, and to Michael Redhill for his overview of my manuscript and encouragement. Not least, my grateful thanks to Daniel Crack for his design work, for his patience, and his devotion to this project.

Prelude

George Eliot says in her novel *Middlemarch*: "We are not afraid of telling over and over again how a man comes to fall in love with a woman and be wedded to her, or else be fatally parted from her."

And so I tell our story, how you and I fell in love, how we wedded, and then what happened. I tell it, too, because I'm still looking for clues about you that escaped me during our marriage. Most of all, I want the world to know about you, what you offered professionally, personally, and about "your little, unremembered acts of kindness and of love." Also, according to William Shakespeare in *Macbeth*, we should "Give sorrow words; the grief that does not speak, knits up the o'er wrought heart and bids it break."

Gordon, you came to me out of the night, a lone figure on silent feet skirting the empty corridors from your door to mine. Now, alone again … as I wander through nights and days, as I sit alone among the embers of my memories, I try to recall how it happened.

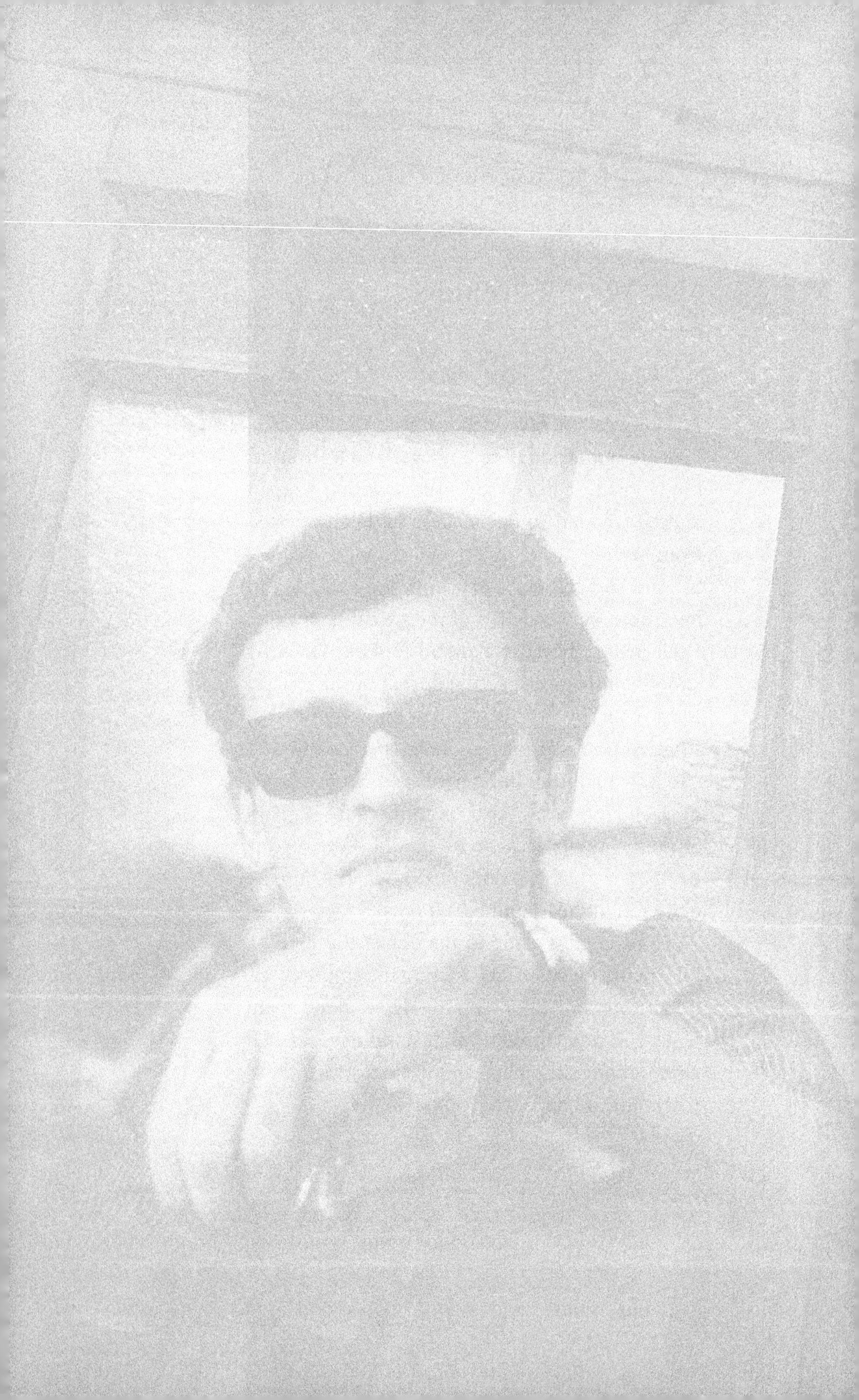

1

In the Beginning

Once, not so very long ago, the person you met and married was a simple matter of geography — how quaint this seems in the age of the Internet and dating sites. But in the upper reach of our lives, you and I walk backward in time; we meet and marry through physical proximity. How improbable after the many decades passed when each of us travels in entirely opposite directions.

It's in 1967 that work takes you to the other end of the earth. In that same year, I wing my way north from New Zealand to Toronto with my first husband and baby. We're criss-crossing each other in the skies. Then, after several years roaming about Southeast Asia, you head to the most distant northerly reaches of British Columbia while I, with my husband and two small children, fly south to New York City. Eventually, each of us moves to various places within Toronto, and in time, become unhitched from our previous spouses. We continue to remain physically far removed from each other.

Our stars begin to align as the years accumulate and we grow older. Eventually, my husband, T., and I sell our house in Pickering and prepare to move into a new condo. But it's not yet completed, so we rent a house in Toronto's Riverdale neighbourhood on the same street where your sister, Mary, lives. We're getting closer. I don't see or meet you there, but we end up on the same floor of the same condo building in the city's Distillery District at more or less the same time. Is this randomness? A fluke? Someone's design?

But it will be many months, perhaps a year or more, before we meet each other, before we love. Before we marry. Before you die.

Sometimes now in my mind I hover above 80 Mill Street in awe of the millions of coincidences and chance circumstances that drew us there to the very same floor at the very same time.

It happens like this. The beginning of a new millennium dawns, and T. and I purchase a condo penthouse unit at one end of a new building in the Distillery District. For financial reasons, we relinquish our house on Berkeley Street, move to a small townhouse in Pickering and then back again to Toronto — a pair of nomads, I'd thought at the time. T. hands me the brochure he's been turning over in his hands. I read that an old whiskey factory and grain mill are being resurrected as condos and commercial buildings by the lake.

"Could be interesting," I say. And almost without thought, we purchase a unit on the penthouse level in one of the three condos built. Immediately, I'm enchanted with the idea of this remaking of a historic site, with the collection of Victorian buildings ribboned through with cobblestone streets, with its first indie shops, coffee lounges, restaurants, and artists' studios. In my mind, I see art lovers trek to galleries that will surely open, music lovers head to open-air concerts. Outdoors, locals and the curious will wander among giant sculptures.

Both of us like the unit, the views, and we think to stay there forever.

T. and I each own a car. This is important because T. must feel free to haunt his golf course — or any course — without hindrance. Also, we must have our own means of transportation, since we live our lives more or less separately, each having long wandered far from each other along different paths — if we'd ever walked the same one. We never tire of the spectacular views from our many windows that face both the city to the northwest, and south over the lake. We like being close to downtown and to the lake, and that within a few minutes we can be in the Distillery District itself with all its amenities. Really, what's not to like?

But it's not long before we feel the need for additional space. T. wants to expand his bedroom into an office or studio, so we purchase the small unit alongside ours.

Do I imagine new beginnings for the two of us? If I think about it at all, I suppose I'll create new patterns or new rhythms to my life, because, hey, it's even a new century. T. will be on the golf course every day, all day, take photos, and play around on his computer. I will read, write, play tennis, and give parties.

In reality, little of this is possible with my husband of two decades or more. I think of all the unhappy times that have rolled by one after another, truces among the conflicts. A new building, a new start in the later years of our lives. No, it's not exactly a new start to our relationship but perhaps a new ability to tolerate each other: T. to live the way he wants in his own separate, cloistered area, I in mine, each pointed in different directions. I've reached the stage where, in the abstract, I like stating I have a husband, but only if I don't actually have to produce him.

One day, I see a tall, thin man emerge from a unit near the elevators at the far end of our condo. I come to know that it's you, Gordon Watts. I judge you to be about my age — T. is older — and think: *This is good. Here's someone in the building with whom we might want to socialize.* I suppose you to have a wife or partner, but repeatedly catch sight of you emerging from your unit alone. Next, I see you at condo board meetings acting as chairman. I watch. I listen to you. I like what I come to know of you. Eventually, I meet you, but only to make small talk in the corridor.

I'll learn later that you, too, believe this will be your final destination, that with your expertise you'll be involved in the management of the building and elected to its board of directors. Eventually, you tell me that with this nearness to downtown you can walk to business meetings, to the St. Lawrence Market on Saturdays, to meet a friend for coffee. No doubt as I do, you'll imagine workers in an earlier time treading the cobblestones; owners weaving among the old brick buildings where workers once toiled in malting factories, grain mills, distilleries. Here you'll live into your old age alone, not looking for love.

Little do either of us imagine that our lives, unsought, will swing full circle in ways unrecognizable to all our earlier selves, to be totally upended — all because we arrive at the same place at the same time, you at one end of a long corridor, I at the other.

People often remark that life can take sudden, unexpected turns.

You make plans, visualize your life flowing along a certain path. You watch it unfolding, slowly, undramatically, your habits already formed, routines established. You suppose these patterns will continue, until suddenly you turn a corner, make a sidestep, or someone sidesteps you. In a split second, everything changes, and you swing around in an entirely different direction. As Annie Baker says in her play *Circle Mirror Transformation*, "do you ever wonder how many times ... your life is gonna totally change and then you'll start all over again?"

New patterns. New routines. You, Gordon, often remarked on this swing in direction with wonder, with exultation.

Infinite times over the months and years in my mind, I walk that long corridor between us, play in it with my toddler granddaughters. Later, much later, it will become the corridor of my restlessness, as in the poem by Ian Thomas Shaw that appears at the beginning of this memoir: "I will meet you at the empty door ... walk the corridors of restlessness ..." Repeatedly, endlessly in my mind, I see myself walking between those walls with my earlier self. In my later dreams and memories, that condo corridor represents in a strange way the long corridor of my life travelled thus far, culminating in the most magnificent years of my life — with you, Gordon Watts.

2

The Man at the Other End of the Corridor

A year and a half passes before I'm aware of you sliding in and out of your condo. You appear to me to be a shy man with a quiet air about you. Vaguely, I notice you're not particularly well dressed, though I come to see that you have some nice clothes but often don't know how to put them together, as if you'd never known how. You get it right here and there, as later I see in old photos. You're not dynamic, not immediately personable. Soft-spoken. All the same, I think, *How attractive.*

Yes, a tall, slight figure — that's my first image. You carry your head slightly forward, and when you look at me, you appear shy and self-conscious. A different, confident you emerges when you preside at board meetings. Alert to all that's being said, razor-like, you cut through the nonsense — and there's much. It's not long before I find myself beginning to watch for you, to catch glimpses of you walking the building's corridors.

You never see me. Not when I come and go. Not when I entertain my granddaughters in those corridors, lining up dolls and teddy bears against the walls to serve as an audience for our soccer games. Not when we kick a rubber ball the length of the corridor and back.

More consciously now, I look for you, tantalized about what's going on inside the tall, thin figure of you. I do sense in you an equanimity, calmness, a quiet intelligence. I try to provoke your shy smile, wondering if perhaps it's a retreat of sorts, as though to protectively hide yourself. As a neighbour will one day say, "I sensed Gordon was a very shy man, even when he appeared to be outgoing."

I realize you probably don't have a wife or partner when repeatedly you come out your door alone. Now, after it's all over, hazy memories of you come to me. Condo board meetings with you. Local political meetings at the pub on Queen Street to the north. A drink afterward. Your smile that lights up your deep-set blue eyes.

"Come to dinner with us," I say one day. "Bring a partner, a friend with you."

"No one comes to mind," you say but seem pleased to accept, and eat ravenously after you arrive. I've seated you at the round glass table with your back against the north wall to give you the best view over the lake. You don't look, only at me, and when catching my eye, immediately lower yours. That evening I treat you as a king and ask what else I can get for you. Intelligence shines from those vanishing blue eyes as we discuss the condo, local politics, the world.

"You really like this guy, don't you?" T. asks me later.

"Yes, very much," I answer immediately, innocently.

In December 2005, your mother dies. It affects you deeply. She might have been ninety-four, ninety-five, but I'll discover she was the woman you most loved in your life. I send you a sympathy card, invite you to dinner. Again, comes that expression of shyness that makes me want to protect you, to warm up what I sense is a shivering soul. Perhaps this is but a small step to wanting to love you. Once more come images of you as a lone figure standing in a desert storm, not buffeted or hurt by it, but wrapped tightly within yourself, strong and contained despite what's thrown at you, withdrawn from you — or not given to you.

In June 2006, I fly to New Zealand to my mother's funeral. It's midwinter. I live in my mother's house, forgetting how very cold and damp it is here. Frost lies heavily on the grass, and houses and shops are as cold indoors as out. But people lunch at sidewalk restaurants under patio heaters wearing short-sleeved shirts.

T. joins me afterward, but before leaving Toronto, asks you to water our plants. "Feel free to borrow our car while we're away," he says.

I return after two months, T. having already done so. I resume my old life: researching, writing and editing. Socializing. Residents and business meetings. I watch for you, at the same time not entirely aware I'm doing this. Vaguely, I hope you'll notice me. However inchoate my longing, I feel your reserve, and intuit that for you to have a friendship or an intimate relationship with me — with anyone — is far from your consciousness, perhaps simply because you don't know how to make it happen.

What I do know is that both of us are disenchanted with board meetings at 80 Mill Street. As an engineer, you're frustrated at the problems the builders have left behind, exasperated with the ignorance of some of the people in the building.

"You might want to join the Corktown Board," I suggest eventually. "You could represent both local residents and the business community. You'll really like them. They're — well, eccentric people," I say teasingly.

We walk there together. I try to get you to notice me but fail, or so I think. "Oblivious," your son, Matt, will say later with annoyance in his voice. All the same, vaguely, I begin to sense in you possible other futures sliding toward me, the hazy sliver of a new dawn, even though I'm married and not consciously intending to be unhitched.

3

Are You Available?

On my bed with the white counterpane, a pale afternoon sun dipping through the windows facing west, I summon those years. Urgently, I search for memories, fearing if I don't find them now, I'll never retrieve the details of how we found each other, especially from such pedestrian beginnings. My mind grabs slivers of memories: an invitation to a local movie, coffee in a Distillery café, local political meetings, a drink in the Dominion Pub afterward. What eludes me still is how we reached that exultant place of love. My need to know is urgent, the missing threads a torment. And I can't quite believe that you, Gordon, came to love me so immediately, so absolutely. Is love in older age sweeter perhaps than anytime before? Is the shape of it different?

And so our beginnings remain a blur and not remarkable, but over days and weeks, I become bewitched by you, by how tall and straight you stand, how unconscious you are of yourself in the world and in relation to it. I think that if all the men in a room are wearing black suits and you're in brown or blue, you'll scarcely notice.

I'm back in memory, recalling an evening where we're returning from a distant meeting. As we walk in from the parking lot, I ask, "Would you like to see around our apartment?" You expressed interest in it upon learning that we purchased the adjoining condo to enlarge the one we had. To date, you've only been downstairs.

"Where's T.?" you ask.

I shrug. "No idea. Probably on a golf course." Later in our conversation, I add that T. spends more and more time in South Africa, and that sometime, he'd like to go back to live close to where he grew up.

As I show you around, I indicate two separate spaces. "We're like roommates," I say, "and not very good ones at that." My husband's bedroom, bathroom, and office are separate and private. It's large and full of windows with spectacular views over the city and lake. Mine is like a platform to nowhere: no doors, no privacy, my bed, a dresser, a desk, open at the top of the stairs. You look but make no comment — only long afterward.

By now, the two of us have more or less become companions. T. has returned from another holiday in South Africa. This early fall day, you and I have just walked back from King Street and have seated ourselves in a quiet corner of a patio in the Distillery to have coffee. Suddenly, I see T. bearing down on us, a spectre looming through the crowds. I interpret a particular facial expression and wonder if he now wants to claim something that in his mind he already rejected. Many who know us will say he completely lost me many years before. But now, intuiting a real threat that I might have gone already, he decides he wants me, after all.

T. sees us, sits down, and we make small talk. Suddenly, with violence, he pushes back his chair, gets up, and tells me I should come home.

I sit there, astonished at his outburst and embarrassed that you witnessed it. I've long wanted out of this marriage. Why haven't I done so before? Fear of many things I know many women will recognize. Being alone. A woman without a husband or partner. Poverty, because two can live more cheaply than one. Having long been in this much-dead marriage, I realize that perhaps, subconsciously, I've been looking to escape it, maybe simply to find friendship, to encounter a particular special connection with another.

A day passes and another. T. comes in late one afternoon. A quarrel ensues between the two of us. Its sources are cloudy, but the words remain clear. In the manner of a little boy, T. says, "Do what you want. I don't care. I've put a down payment on a condo outside Johannesburg near a golf course, so there!"

South Africa, the country of T.'s origins. A place where the sun always shines. And a golf course. Those things figure. But still I'm shocked.

"What am I supposed to do?" I ask.

"You can wait for me here and I'll come back maybe about every six months."

"Then this has to be the end of us," I say.

4

Will You Marry Me?

Late one afternoon, you and I are again seated across from each other at a small table in a courtyard in the Distillery. T. has taken another holiday in South Africa. We are there among the ghosts of those who long ago toiled in the grime and dust beneath old stone walls. Then, suddenly, you lean forward. Your whole body is alight, and a warm sky mirrors the blue of your eyes. Your smile for me is a particular one, and I look at you in wonder. I notice the long, lean swoop of you with your curly white hair and those lambent eyes all but hidden under your massive eyebrows. It's when I notice urgency in your posture and expression that I get a vague sense of some different kind of future sliding toward me.

The air about us becomes hushed. The crowds have vanished. I feel the two of us to be alone among the old stone walls under a deepening sky. Scattered sunlight flickers over you and spangled air dances on cobblestones where shadows are already creeping. I feel those ancient walls rise up to tower about us, sense the cobblestones beneath our feet, warm and rough. I smile as I look at you, riveted by a conviction that something momentous is about to happen. Your eyes hold mine as you slide onto one knee, your smile warm, gentle, but with strong purpose.

"I would like to become your third husband," you say, your eyes not leaving mine, "that is, if you will have me."

Oh-oh! The first inkling of the measuring, quantitative person you are comes to me. Suddenly inarticulate, I watch as out of your jeans pocket you withdraw a small object — not a ring, but a notebook. You hand it to me. On its pink cover are the words "The First Two Husbands Were Just for Practice."

"Oh! Really?" Something huge, wild, improbable swells within me, but before I can answer, you repeat, "If you will have me." I know by the intense light in your eyes that you're certain of my reply.

Later, much later after it's all over, after the inexpressible joy of those ten, eleven years, and the tragedy that ended it, I replay this scene over and over. I conjure two figures in sharp silhouette, you kneeling on cobblestones, and as vividly as I did then, I see your deep-set eyes lit up, and again feel as though I'm falling into them. I'm leaning forward, hearing you say not *Will you marry me?* but *I would like to become your third husband, that is, if you will have me.*

Inarticulate yearning flashes in your eyes as you wait for my reply, a longing for love that perhaps you've never felt, except from your mother. And here we are: I, seeing love brimming from you and snatching at it, taking it into the coldness that has long inhabited my heart. I think, *How beautiful you are*, there among those ghosts of long ago, and you so soon to be one, too, but this, mercifully, we are not yet to know.

Then, suddenly, I see myself, a woman not young, but perhaps arresting with a slim form and colourful clothes. A woman intensely alive with quick movements and a certain restlessness about her. She's looking momentarily astonished, then the light that touches her face becomes equal to the intensity in his. But he also has a hungry look. She glances at him, then away, startled, overwhelmed and not expecting this — well, not so soon.

Still intently searching my memories, I see again the slow sparking of a fire between us that will quickly illuminate everything around us. You, on the outside, as your sister said of you when younger, might be perceived as nerdy, awkward, shy. But it seems an easy thing for me to find your shimmering soul hidden beneath your exterior and set it aflame — for me. *For me.*

I never want to pull myself out of that memory and repeatedly summon it, to see again how you take that notebook out of your pocket, the words on it coming back to me. I see myself jumping to my feet, grabbing your hands, pulling you to your feet. Leaning close to you, I whisper, "Yes, yes, and yes!"

"Yes, yes, and yes!" I repeat now, and in my reverie, perceive a collision of past and present, a glorious future fixed for me. I'm trying to hold on to that recollection, to discern other details, but much of it is elusive. That corridor between us, you at one end, I at the other. If walls could share what they heard, what they saw, they'd tell of small children laughing as they kicked a soccer ball along its length, small dogs from the neighbouring condo joining in. They'd also speak of early mornings when you, shoes in one hand, walk on silent feet from my door to yours. You in our apartment, I in yours. Suddenly, we're going to be together.

I glimpse the glorious haze of our future, discern unending vistas stretching before us in that never-ending future.

Your proposal of marriage has come swiftly and seemingly out of nowhere.

T. attempts to claim what he lost long ago, and I feel ragged pity for him.

"No," I tell him. "I'm sorry. It's too late."

I've never been more certain of anything in all the decades of my life, even though friends say, "Hey, you've done this twice before."

"I know. I don't care. I want this."

But what really did I know of you, Gordon, that I should leap seemingly so precipitously into a permanent relationship with you? And as a friend reminded me, "You've already had two husbands." A leap of faith? Third time lucky? Maybe hope over experience?

I say to anyone who wants to know that everything about you is readily available: you're a mining engineer, a computer scientist, a mathematician, an entrepreneur and consultant with your own company. You have a son in his forties who's an artist, and an ex-wife from long ago. You're the oldest of six siblings whom you love. You're unattached. You want to travel.

And you love me and want to marry me!

I particularly absorb that you love travelling, and in your twenties, you moved through Asia during the Vietnam War, through Australia, Singapore, Malaysia, Indonesia, Japan, Nepal, Cambodia, Thailand, and Tibet. And I imagine you as a young man rambling alone in remote places for years and think, *What does that say about you?* I'll ask you about it, but not yet, not in our first days, weeks, months together. I'm too busy imagining our world in the present and beyond this wild blush of romance.

5
We Are Us

It's July 2007 when T. and I sell our condo. Before I leave for the last time, I wander about that empty space — a palace I once thought, now with walls stained with acrimony and disappointment, with hurt and disengagement, with nothing in the end. I lean on a windowsill and gaze at the magnificent view to the north. Clouds, heavy all day, have lifted. A sun-spotted cityscape emerges, and turning, I see the lake bronzed in late-afternoon sunlight. Joy at the thought of you waiting for me flits through me until I feel I'm rising, lifting off to some beautiful unknown.

After that comes a flurry of joyful decision-making. I, still married, you in a hurry, a loved-starved man. A man who has always prized his own company and sought little of others has been awakened to the possibility, the idea and the reality of love, of like-minded companionship — a heady mix.

We'll get married! It's like a shout to the universe.

We'll buy a house.

We'll furnish it together.

We'll have children.

"We're how old?" you ask.

We both laugh.

"We'll have six," I say. "Don't you think that's a good number?"

And so we talk and dream.

6

Together

We're going to be together. We need a home. One balmy midsummer day I drive to Cabbagetown to see a friend on Berkeley Street where once T. and I lived until his crazy investment schemes floundered and we had to move, not sideways but downward. I loved that street, romanticized it, imagined it as it once was. I remain enchanted with it still. All those years before I wrote short stories and set them there. Today, it's as I remember it: sunlight filtering among shadows cast by the soaring branches of giant chestnut trees. Small front gardens elaborately staged. Houses, Victorian beauties with decorative trim and sloping eaves.

After my visit to this venerable lady in her large red brick home opposite the one T. and I owned, I'm about to slide into my car when the voice of a neighbour beckons me to join him for a drink.

"The house next door's for sale," he says. "Why don't you buy it?"

Berkeley Street. In my dreams, in my imagination, in my fiction, I see it again: Victorian houses crowded stiffly against one another like strangers rubbing elbows. A Union Jack hanging from Pimblett's Queen's Head Pub on the corner. A faded portrait of the queen in drag from atop the third floor.

This day, as I stand poised on the sidewalk, familiar sounds come back to me: the clanging of wrought-iron gates and the tapping of heels on pavement. The roaring of car engines into life. The judge's dog barking in frenzy as his master's bandy legs carry him to a waiting limousine.

But as Eden is often spoiled, so, too, are parts of Cabbagetown. I won't deny it has challenges. I've walked laneways littered with discarded condoms, among winos unconscious on someone's doorstep. Others piss up against the side of a laneway house, and now I remember the old gentleman living there and how he installed a water fountain to mask the sounds of life lived right beside him, honeysuckle to overpower the smells. But that was many years earlier; Cabbagetown has much improved.

At this moment, I feel it must be ordained that I return here. Immediately, I phone you, then make an appointment for us to see it. What a shock we get when we enter — it's filthy. Coffee stains its walls. The smell of rotting carpets pervade the empty spaces. For more than three years, garbage has accumulated in the basement and garage. The backyard is lush with weeds clambering over the disintegrating wooden patio, threatening to march through the sliding glass doors into the sunroom.

We don't care about any of this; we can fix it.

"I feel lost in here," you say.

"Hah! It won't take me long to find you."

A narrow Victorian, it has three floors and a full basement, and within its twenty-four hundred square feet of space is a large entry hall, an elongated living room, a dining room, a powder room, kitchen, and a sunroom leading to a potentially beautiful garden and garage that opens out to a laneway. Upstairs has three bedrooms, two bathrooms. Then there's a beautiful third-floor room with skylights. This will become your office.

We begin intense efforts to clean, scrub, remove old wallpaper, to throw out stained carpets. Then follow visits to wood, furniture, and appliance stores, to paint shops and rug emporiums. We are a young/old couple embarking on a life.

Even before we've properly cleaned and furnished the house the way we like, we entertain our friends and families. We plan a wedding.

7

A Wedding

The day comes when I prepare to become a bride for the third time, and what follows is a lot of joyful decision-making. We smile at each other often, and if noticing, don't care about — even admire — fine wrinkles circling our wrists, the greying hair, the slackening jaws, the sunspots and other evidence of many decades of life already lived. We will promise ourselves to each other, to love each other for all eternity.

Someone asks me why we're marrying.

"Just for the convenience of introducing you," I say at once, laughing, "what am I supposed to call him? A partner? That suggests a business relationship. My boyfriend? Really? We're in our sixties. My significant other? Are you kidding? Oh, I suppose I could call him my sidekick. I'm marrying him so I can call him my husband."

For me, marriage is a public declaration of a serious commitment to another. I want the world to know I love you, and you, me. Both of us intend to sustain this marriage until death splits us apart. Fancifully, I conjure images where we'll take our relationship out every morning and polish it up. In the evening, hold it up and admire it.

Avalanches of words have been written about marriage, and after being asked what this ancient institution is, I think of George Eliot's passage in *Middlemarch*:

> The fact is unalterable, that a fellow-mortal with whose nature you are acquainted solely through the brief entrances and exits of a few imaginative weeks called courtship, may, when seen in the continuity of married companionship, be disclosed as something better or worse than what you have preconceived, but will certainly not appear altogether the same.

Or as the seventeenth-century American poet Edward Taylor remarks in "Upon Wedlock, and Death of Children":

A curious Knot God made in Paradise,
    And drew it out inamled neatly fresh.
It was the True-Love Knot, more sweet than spice
    And set with all the flowres of Graces dress.
    Its Weddens Knot, that ne're can be unti'de.
    No Alexanders Sword can it divide.

Exactly: it cannot, and will not, be divided, except in death, and how soon death comes!

In a discussion about relationships, I recall someone declaring that without arguments or fights, the needs of one partner in the relationship aren't being met. I think about this, and eventually quote it to you.

"I think that at our age," you say, "we should be mature enough to resolve any differences without resorting to fighting."

King Solomon's wisdom, indeed.

Often, I summon memories. Myself in a creamy silk sari with crimson-laced accents, my many bridesmaids in multicoloured saris, my daughter and granddaughters in Punjabi suits. You waiting for me on the wide verandah wearing a dark blue suit and polished shoes, your hair slicked back. That hair — I remember the countless times I've run my hands through it to ruffle and mess it up. Looking taller than your six feet, slim as a sapling oak, you stand with shoulders raised. It's when you turn and look at me that the lyrics of an old song come to me:

> I might be right, and I might be wrong
> But I'm perfectly willing to swear
> The night you turned and smiled at me
> A nightingale sang in Berkeley Square.

Maybe not Berkeley Square, but Berkeley Street will do. We glitter in the garden of my friend, Maria, who offers up her beautiful home for our celebration. Through the giant oaks in the garden filter the words of New Zealand's famous Māori love song, "Pokarekare Ana," sung by Kiri Te Kanawa. Only afterward do the portent of those words translated into English hit me:

> They are agitated,
> the waters of Waiapu,
> But when you cross over girl,
> they will be calm.
>
> Oh girl
> return to me,
> I could die
> of love for you.
>
> I could die for love of you ... no!

Notes from Handel's Trumpet Concerto, pompous and elegant, also seem to drop from those trees to soar above them. What kind of speech will you make? I wonder, thinking you're not really the speech-making type. Lost to me is much of it, but I register the words: "Carolyn has an enthusiasm for life you seldom see in anyone over fourteen years old. She's the easiest person in the world to live with, beautiful, accomplished ..." Certainly not beautiful. Accomplished? I can't think of anything except maybe my three books of non-fiction published a long time ago.

"I'm her third husband, and I'm the lucky one ..." As I hear you say this, I understand with the certainty of a person who believes the sun will rise, the moon in its night sky, that your devotion will be constant, permanent until ... until ...

When my turn comes to find words to explain you, I repeat what I've said before, that you're the most beautiful man the world can hold, brilliant and humble, a man without an ego as Maria's late husband said of you. You're a non-hierarchical person who enjoys your own company. A man who walks to your own drummer — but more of that later.

I joke when I say, "A successful marriage requires the falling in love many times, but always with the same person." And "A girl must marry for love and keep on marrying until she finds it."

And so the first two husbands were just for practice.

I might also have added a quote from *Wuthering Heights* when Cathy says about Heathcliff to Nelly, the main narrator of the novel: "Whatever our souls are made of, his and mine are the same."

My granddaughters recite Edward Lear's poem "The Owl and the Pussy-Cat" whose characters, at the end of their long journey, say, "Oh, let us be married ... too long we have tarried ... and hand in hand by the edge of the sand, they danced by the light of the moon ..."

• • •

After the wedding, we drive to our house on Berkeley Street. It's that vision of a door that comes back to me when I say to my new husband: "Will you carry me over the threshold?" And to our new/old house we return, I still dreaming I'm in a fairy tale, a dream from which I never want to awake in this life — or any other.

But that door, the entrance to a whole new life, will in the end become the empty door of my nightmares, and a searing emptiness that will follow me the rest of my life.

Now, on the matrimonial bed where I stretch out to summon you, I see myself in my exquisite sari, jewels in my hair, see you with lambent eyes bending toward me, and I think about the dreams and fantasies spoken in this bedroom of ours and how, all the while out the windows, clouds shift over the chestnut trees, half blocking the view of high-rises. How that world rolls on and people work and sleep and laugh and fight. I'm on that bed where first we loved, then we slept, if we did, where we floated together in a single dream, once more hearing you ask, "So how many kids will we have?"

"I think we've already discussed this, but okay, let's have six."

"Well, maybe that's too many since we're ... how old?"

"Forty-five."

We both laugh.

Every love needs witnesses, it's said, approval from the outside world in the newly merged union of two. Yes, the world must have lovers because only they, in the monotony of everyday life, show how it's really different, that "It's better than it's used to thinking of itself ..."

8

Who Are You?

"Really, how well do you know the man you just married?" When this statement is repeated, I think about what I know of you, your beginnings and their influences, your early environment and what impact it had on you and your world view. (Fleetingly, I think about the unknowability of anyone, and do we even know ourselves?)

This is what I do know. The first of six siblings, you, Gordon Daniel

Taylor Watts, are born to Marjorie and Murray Watts at home in a tiny bungalow in Malartic in the remote Val d'Or region of northwestern Quebec on June 27, 1942. This small town of three thousand people perches precipitously on the edge of a prosperous gold mine near Noranda. I think about your intrepid mother who, in quick succession, gives birth after you to Murray, then Mary. Later, Robert, Muriel, and David follow. I ask how she survived the long, punishing winters and primitive conditions.

"Unfazed" is what I hear from you.

Northwestern Quebec is a place of low-lying forests where ridges are criss-crossed by creeks. A place of swamp and shallow valleys. I've seen photos of the tracks of old exploration activities of the 1930s and after, and think that even as small boy, you might have had a kind of subterranean consciousness of the closeness of one of the largest gold-mining areas in the world — Abitibi Greenstone Belt.

If there's a collective unconscious, if there's somehow a genetic passing on of profound emotional experiences, then your father's work must also have influenced you. Murray Watts Senior was an intrepid adventurer and explorer, a mining engineer with a particular passion for rare minerals of the earth and the challenges of mining them. He's credited with the discovery of the Raglan Hill Deposits and the Asbestos Hill Mine. And it's his finding of the world-class Mary River iron ore deposits on Baffin Island that resonates today, since it represents the most significant undeveloped high-grade iron ore resource on the planet, now being exploited.

Paternal influence and example would have been plentiful, and there's much written and known about your father, perhaps best known for his work in the North. There, his large number of major iron ore discoveries revealed much about that vast land inside the Arctic Circle. Besides the already mentioned finds, he's noted for recognizing the value of the Vestron zinc-lead deposits in Greenland. Not the least, he was the founder of "47"-zone copper in the Coppermine River area of the Northwest Territories, as well as determining the value of fluorite, tin, and tungsten at Lost River in Alaska.

Endless are the stories about him, the following but a few:

- His twelve-hundred-mile canoe journey into Quebec's Ungava region from Ontario's Moose Factory at the southern end of James Bay.
- His part in the construction of more than a dozen airstrips within the Arctic Circle, one of the first to recognize the low costs of sea shipments and the use of large aircraft to provide inexpensive unit-cost structures in Far North mineral exploration.
- His innovative use of enormous four-engine Hercules aircraft to support his Coppermine exploration project.
- His becoming mine superintendent for Canadian Malartic Gold Mines, then chief engineer and eastern manager for contractor Patrick Harrison, and later, general manager for Little Long Lac Gold Mines.

The Arctic and its exploration were your father's realms. He had a true love for Canada's North, and often when at home at the dinner table with his six children, in his mind he was always there. Abstractly, he'd stare into the distance, not hearing or seeing the family life around him. Then, with a sudden leap from his chair, he'd rush to the phone and yell into it: "There's a jutting piece of rock at the southern edge of Mary Lake." (Named after his daughter, Mary). "Get there. Take samples. Now!" This man's thoughts were on cold, distant granite and other rocks in isolated spots of the planet that potentially hid what might be massive mineral wealth. Your father was awarded the Order of Canada, as well as the Massey Medal of the Canadian Geographical Society.

Like your father, like your brothers, each in their own way, you searched out and accepted physically challenging conditions, struggled and endured privation in the pursuit of your work. I wonder if you would have followed mining engineering if your father's influence hadn't been there.

• • •

You, Gordon, originally enrolled in geology at the University of Toronto but switched at the end of your first year to mining engineering. Not surprising, I suppose, since you so enjoyed discovering how things work, the mysteries in the earth, the astronomical secrets of the heavens and the cosmos. Your bedtime reading included physics, a history of calculus and how it changed the world. Also Herodotus's *The Histories*. Much later came manuals on data analysis and business modelling.

In the many hours and days after you've gone, I lie on our bed and summon events you recounted to me, memories, and the stories I've been told about you. Memories? Perhaps it's retelling that becomes memory. Images pile on one another. Unending and bone-chilling winters in your mother Marjorie's primitive home in Malartic. No running water, little heat. Each child painstakingly dressed in snowsuits, mittens, hats, scarves, in preparation for sending them out into the Arctic cold. Minutes later, Marjorie, having just closed the door, hears, "Mommy, I need to go to the bathroom." The process of undressing, then redressing is repeated all over again.

"My poor mother," you tell me, smiling at private recollections. Of all her children, you as a baby, and throughout your life, are the most loved by her as many first-born children often are. When a toddler, she puts you outside to play with other small children. Happily, you do so, but keep returning to the door to check that she's within sight and sound. This is recorded in the baby book she kept for you that I now have in my possession. This love from your mother, and yours for her, endures as primary and all-encompassing.

Your family moves to Leaside in Toronto when you're eight years old, Murray seven, Mary six, and Robert four. You, Murray, and Robert share a tiny bedroom with bunk beds, your younger brother, Robert, with a small bed wedged against the opposite wall.

You tell me how much you loved those years in this middle-class neighbourhood, and I imagine that small house rocking with the shrieks of five children who also take over local streets and haunt the shops on Bayview Avenue. Who, in winter, skate and toboggan frozen patches of ice. Whenever we drive north — and most areas of the city are to the north of us — you'll head to this area of Leaside, happily, nostalgically, pointing out your old primary school, the skate-sharpening shop, the barbershop, the old movie theatre, all of which remain except the last, which has been reincarnated for another use.

Memories are told by brothers and sisters about Saturday movies, ten cents per show, about that house, impossibly small and overstuffed with kids. "Five of them now," Marjorie says, not intending to have more. Then comes David, almost eighteen years after you, Gordon. When later David asks his mother why she married his dad, she says, "All I wanted was to raise a family."

I'm upstairs in your chair, my darling, looking at photos, thinking about your young life, about your brother, Murray, who told me how you shared a bedroom.

"I was nine, Gordon ten," Murray says. "I've set myself to do homework. I'm pretty well organized and get myself prepared for the next day — hockey equipment, homework, my clothes set out because I get up early. Then lights out and I'm into bed. Gordon comes in, switches on the light, and gets ready to begin his homework."

I know that you, Gordon, won't, or maybe can't, even attempt sleep until the night has waned and morning light creeps in the windows. When your sister, Mary, repeats Murray's story, I see images of you squished on your bed, papers, books, charts scattered about you, a happy scene of chaos.

Then comes St. Michael's School in Toronto where you continue to ace all your subjects. But your diurnal rhythm remains out of whack with your brothers and sisters, perhaps with the world, and it's a problem. You're the one with the driver's licence responsible for getting your siblings to school on time. Murray, Mary, and Muriel wait in the car in the driveway, neat, homework prepared. You run out the door, a half-eaten piece of toast in one hand, your school bag in the other, and somehow at the same time, you yank at your crooked shirt tie. The three of you, always late, find yourselves in the principal's office to explain things.

While you're all in elementary school, your indomitable mother prepares lunch for the first four of you who return home for it, then reads to you, books such as *Robinson Crusoe* and *Little Women*. Reading — yes, that fits.

You're in a pew at Blessed Sacrament Church on Sundays and every day during Lent — really! I laugh when you tell me that. In reality, as a teenager, instead of attending the local Catholic church with the family, you and Mary tell your mother you're attending another church, and the two of you slip off to a restaurant for lunch. You become agnostic, a sometime atheist — who ever knows the heart of another, I even of yours? Despite the knowledge I have of you, in some parts of you, dear Gordon, you are unknowable.

Such is a sketch of your early life. Fragmented accounts of your university years come to me from your friends, Tom Horsley and Lee Barker, which I include, but little about your twenties when you travel throughout Asia.

With me, as you've done in high school and more than a half century later, you don't change your nighttime habits. Perhaps a person can't. I, a lifelong insomniac, am in bed, trying to go to sleep … well, I dream of it, thinking that one day, or I should say one night, I'll manage it. You come down the stairs from the third floor, never in a hurry, and into the bedroom to my side of the bed. You bend over and kiss me. Your lips are damp, a sloppy kiss. I love that unfailingly you do this those nights I go to bed before you.

Oh, for the intimacies of a deeply shared life! I love all of you, even when you're swaying back and forth from one leg to the other while talking to me. "Good for balance," you say. You're there at the end of the bed while I relax on it as you recount alluring tales of old adventures, about the state of the world, about what you're reading.

"Hey," I ask, "could you do that afterward? That swaying thing makes me dizzy."

Was I unfairly critical? You, this man I married, has no conceit about himself, no thought of how he appears to the world. Do you think about how you look to yourself, Gordon?

Sometimes you'll come out of the bathroom and say, "I peered in the mirror and thought, *Who's that old man staring back at me?*"

"Couldn't be you," I say, laughing. "Come here, old man."

Never mind the past. Whatever it's made up of, you came to me as you are now with whatever formed you, and I love the entire package of you. What you lay at my feet is the whole of you tinged, forged, shaped by a complicated past that one day I'll sort out, that eventually you'll give to me in pieces as you want to.

9

The Pageant of My Universe

I'm in our sunroom in the chair where you always sat, facing a blank television. I'm thinking how immense were those days and nights with you, how we lived our lives in Technicolor. I see the light in your eyes falling on me and remember … Now I'm crying for you as I shop, as I walk, as I make conversation in the middle of a dinner party.

I'm crying right now as I write this, weary, and as in Virginia Woolf's novel *Mrs Dalloway*, I feel like laying my suddenly immensely aged head on the earth and disappearing into it. Like her, I feel that the pageant of my universe will soon be over. But next, I'm in the supermarket carrying out bags of groceries, and suddenly, in the middle of the parking lot, I stop. Is this all just for me? For ten years, I did it all for us — *us*. Now I do everything alone. Then comes that feeling of emptiness I so dread, a cold, hard stone heavy inside me. Do I have to do everything alone for the rest of my life?

"What did you get for me?" you'll ask when I return with the groceries.

I'll pretend I've purchased nothing, then with a flourish, produce your favourite pastry.

10

Patterns Interrupted

Some time after our wedding, you're asked to relocate to Vancouver for three months.

"Three months!" I cry.

"Well, you're coming, too, of course."

"Okay!"

Your friend and colleague, Charles Pitcher, the CEO of Canadian

Western Coal, has hired you. You're to evaluate the company's assets and future earnings in readiness for a request for proposal. This includes establishing a value and cost on production, sales costs, potential profits, future earnings, world markets.

I join you in Vancouver within weeks of your leaving, and we continue our honeymoon in various high-rise condo buildings. You ask me to bring you some particular attachment for your laptop from a computer store called Notebook on Dundas Street East. I remember this, because it's an unlikely place to spook me afterward, but it does. In Vancouver, you work office hours, and afterward and on weekends, we walk the seawall in the West End, roam Stanley Park, the hills above the city and beyond. We talk. We love. Together, we dream our dreams. I don't ask much about your work — formulas, equations, mathematical calculations — because I can't even find the questions to ask.

One day, I recall shopping for groceries in a local supermarket. Busy with my thoughts, I ignore the piped-in music until a few words penetrate and I hear the voice of Debbie Reynolds from the 1950s singing "Tammy":

> Does my lover feel what I feel when he comes near?
> My heart beats so joyfully
> You'd think that he could hear
> Wish I knew if he knew what I'm dreaming of
> Tammy, Tammy, Tammy's in love.

As for many, a tune sometimes so fixates in the brain that it's hard to shut it off, so I ramble about our rented condo crooning the words to this song. You're bemused, amused, so unaccustomed are you to this joyful noise-making.

We have friends and family in Vancouver and do many things together, but it's a pleasure to be home again in Toronto and into a happy routine. One might shrug or dismiss the idea of routine. Often it connotes boredom, sameness, a state of being uninspired and dull. But habit isn't to be despised, and you only realize its value when finding yourself without it. To me, change can enhance the pleasure of any ritual by consecrating its unchanging nature. And so back in Toronto patterns form: breakfast in the sunroom that faces east and warmed by the sun, in the garden in summer, a couple of hours reading the news — but less time for me, the restless, driven one.

It's lunchtime. "I'll make us something," I say.

Then you work, I work. You're on the elliptical machine, then a long time in the shower. "It's where I do all my thinking," you tell me. Then a walk outdoors, some shopping.

I make dinner my responsibility, and you tell me I'd be a good short-order cook because of my ability to put together a dinner within half an hour, often with what I have in the fridge. To you, everything I put on the table is the best and the finest, and you devour it as though I've given you the feast of your lifetime. Sweetie, I loved cooking for you! And I remember how each evening I'd call up the stairs — another routine — "Dinner's ready!"

"I'll be down in a minute," you say. Or "I'm coming." Next thing, your footsteps creak on stairs from the third floor, to the second, to the main floor, across the long corridor and into the kitchen.

Each evening when you enter the kitchen, I exult in the gift of you, the gift of a freshly restored painting, vivid, exhilarating, always new.

"Do you want to watch something tonight?" you ask after dinner. "Or just read?"

"Yes," I answer to both questions, adding, "or go to a pub?" As in shared experiences, thoughts, values, dreams, we're largely of one mind in what we want to do and watch. Occasionally, you turn to science programs such as *A Field Guide to Planets, Biochemistry, Biology and How Life Works, The Big Bang.*

I'm cocooned in the second-floor middle room, my office at the foot of the stairs that lead to your third-floor room. It's dark but not windowless, and three of its walls are lined with books. I love this place, love my books — my friends as I think of them, always looking out at me and wondering which one of them I'll pick up. Our voices float up and down the stairs as we talk about a news item, or an experience triggered by what we've been reading.

You come down the stairs into my office, ask what I'm up to, and listen as though every word I speak is to be remembered forever, everything I do of infinite interest to you. Your vision of me is an intoxicating one, like a mirror held up, and I enjoy how I see myself in it. It's like a rebirth: no matter how many people tell me how beautiful I am (I'm not), how smart (not really), how strong (maybe), it doesn't mean anything. I don't feel loved or wanted when friends, even near-strangers, invite me out and are kind to me. It's only you who make me feel cherished, special, beautiful.

I remain now in memory, hearing myself going about the house singing, hearing you, with joy in your voice, call out from the third floor, "No singing allowed in the house!"

"But this isn't really singing."

Images of the two of us come to me, and I think that our marriage was, and is, like the soaring flame of a candle, only to be snuffed out with suddenness. *Snap*! A bludgeoning. You, dead, I, cut in half, diminished, oh, so diminished. I'm in that sunroom chair, the television silent, the air filled instead with sounds and images of you, with stories told to me about you. You're sent outside by your father, but in the middle of winter with your brother, Murray, to sleep in a tent — a great adventure to Murray but miserable for you. And when the house lights are turned off, you sneak back into it to read by the beam of your flashlight.

"Take him outside for God's sake," your father orders his second son. "Get him out onto the ice, toughen him up. Get him some boxing gloves." All this is joy to the heart of the favoured second son but torture and deprivation to you, Gordon, for you want only to read, to absorb knowledge of the world and everything in it. Reading is and has been your great joy all through your life. I've joked to friends that if you walk through the kitchen on your way to the front door, if there's a cereal box lying on the counter as you pass, you'll stop and read the words written on it. This devotion to reading is anathema to your father who tells you, "If you don't stop reading, you'll rot your brains."

11

Beds We Sleep In

Two months, three — maybe more after you've gone — deliberately, I begin reliving our travels. It's a necessary means of holding on to you, and it comforts me. Untold are the hours and days I spend in my mind moving about the world with you. I continue to roam to all those places we visited, we loved, and left. I particularly enjoy remembering the beds we slept in, spectacular, bizarre, and in between. In my mind, in the many times I've gone around the world, right now I've landed in New Zealand. Over our ten, eleven years together, we made four visits there.

12

New Zealand

"When are we going Down Under?" we eventually ask each other.

"Tomorrow," I say, smiling up at you. "You'll have to meet all my relatives — three sisters and brothers-in-law, thirty-seven first cousins, eighteen nephews and nieces. And three uncles and one aunt. You're sure you still want to go?"

And so I start planning a trip for us to New Zealand, to introduce you to it, and to some of my relatives. I begin dreaming of the place where my family's history is written up in Hansard, is imprinted on the bleached bones of my forebears. This is to be our first visit to the land of my birth, first to stay with my relatives in both Auckland and Hamilton, then just the two of us to cross by ferry to Waiheke Island, which will be our home for three weeks. The second-largest island in the Hauraki Gulf after Great Barrier Island, it lies thirteen miles from downtown Auckland. It was once also my enchanted childhood second home.

We find no accommodation at any reasonable cost, so settle for a tiny shack deep in the bush. I remember the astounded voice of my uncle when he saw it: "How ever could you sleep in that?" And in my mind, I've returned to that particular bed in that shack half hidden up a slope among punga tree ferns and nikau palms on the island. Cautiously, we climb a staircase that's really a ladder in disguise to a tiny loft with a small bed beneath a mosquito net that occupies the entire space. It leaves scarcely elbow room, never mind my restless legs!

Waiheke: every square inch of this little hideaway is alive with bugs, bacteria, and fungi. Plants grow on plants and plants suck on air. A beach of endless bleached sand stretches to a limitless horizon while waves incessantly, tumultuously roll in from the Pacific Ocean.

While on that holiday, you receive an online request for a project that has a short deadline.

"Oh!" I exclaim, recognizing your expression. Even though you're tucked away in bush in the thick haze of an antipodean summer, you look pleased. Now in your seventies, but with your particular expertise, you're still in demand by large companies around the world. On that wraparound verandah with fecund growth trailing over the wooden railings to trip you, your laptop balanced in your hands, you pace, searching for an Internet connection.

"I'll have to drive down to the beach," you say with a hint of frustration. And so we head to one of the two restaurants on the beach that boasts a good Wi-Fi connection. The signals aren't reliable. We then trek to a hilltop to try another location. Lovely views, but again, only a sporadic connection.

But how I enjoy the walk down that meandering dirt road through dense bush rustling with birdlife.

I feel hugely alive.

I feel young.

I feel rich, old, and young again.

I'm in love.

And more than all this, Waiheke Island continues to summon memories of my fairy-tale childhood summers. Both of us love it: the little movie theatre with its ramshackle armchairs and overstuffed couches, its volunteers handing out ice cream as we enter, the summery beach scenes and one-of-a-kind little shops. I can sense your pleasure as you amble the long beach of Onetangi where birds, strange to you, strut the sand and peck with their extraordinarily long, sharp beaks for oysters beneath the sand — oystercatchers by name.

Visions float of another visit two years after this: a beach outside Gisborne on North Island's far-flung east coast. Narrow, creaky beds there, but a lovely location.

The same uncle asks me, "Why ever would you go to an outpost like that?"

"Why? Beautiful beaches," I answer. "Horseback riders galloping in the surf. Dogs and children playing in the waves." Great fishing, I might have added, not that we indulge in the sport, but we're grateful for daily fresh fish offered to us by our hosts. It's a small town but with an international flavour boasting Italian and Turkish restaurants. Also, within a short radius are two small cities: Napier, a coastal art deco town; and Hastings, a wine- and fruit-producing inland place — each with a particular vibe and appeal.

Not easily do you leave the limitless sandy beaches and forested pathways of our various destinations in New Zealand where you walk in the mornings, mid-afternoons, and evenings. Not easily do you relinquish the feeling of warm sand beneath your feet; your study of rare native birds pecking for food beneath that sand, admiring and examining native flora. The physical world — that's what early on you learn to love. But often I wonder if these temperate climes and sunny beaches of the world are but a novelty, your true love being what you know, what's in your blood — the harsh, unforgiving climate of Canada's North, the environment of your early struggles. I say this but learn over our sojourn together that you love and appreciate wherever in the world you are, that you can live anywhere and be happy and are happy within yourself. "Overall a contented man," your son, Matt, once commented.

On yet another visit to New Zealand, we walk the endless pristine beaches along the Coromandel Peninsula, wander golden sands of the northern tip of North Island with its singular, semi-tropical flavour. At the island's most northern tip is a silvery line that marks the divide between the South Pacific and the Tasman Sea, a promontory aloof and lonely. Remote — yes, very!

13
This Is Us

Not long after our return from that first visit, you stand in my office doorway and announce that you have to go to Peru on business. "I thought it could wait a few months," you say, "but they need me there sooner." You look pleased. As before you say, "You could come, too."

"Hey, yes, I could!" What an adventure to be up in the remote mountains of Peru. It doesn't work out that time, and while you're away, I attend Ryerson University courses, writers' groups, and book clubs. When you're home again, we hold dinner parties and are hosted in turn. Randomly, we go to concerts, operas, and movies. Initially, I've perceived you as a solitary person who enjoys your own company, and when concerned I'll crowd you, I quote Rainer Maria Rilke: "I hold this to be the highest task for a bond between two people: that each protects the solitude of the other." And I think to space out our entertainment. But this is what happens.

"I've got us tickets to a Beethoven concert on Saturday night," I announce one mid-weekday. "And Di Thomson and Barry Little are coming for dinner Sunday. Oh, and I almost forgot, we're going to a lecture at Innis College on Tuesday."

You embrace it all with enthusiasm, and often at the end of a week, ask, "So what's on for this weekend?"

"Oh, actually not much." I'm wandering about with a duster in my hand. "Housework, ugh!"

You seem disappointed at the lack of social activity.

"Gordon always enjoyed social occasions," your sister, Mary, says, "but he just didn't know how to make them happen."

One whole summer on Friday afternoons, you come with me to the University of Toronto where Victor Ostapchuk, associate professor of

Middle Eastern studies, meets with his Ph.D. students. Each one presents research findings on the history of various tribes and regions of sixteenth-century Turkey. I ask, "Who would choose to spend hot Friday afternoons listening to what are ultimately dry recitations on obscure subjects?"

You would.

Why would you? Innate curiosity, of course, and to be with me.

"Hey, a free organ recital at the Metropolitan United Church. I love organ music." I announce this one Thursday winter morning. Immediately, you say you'll come, too. We step outside into a world of gently falling snow, each flake as large as a rose petal. As we walk, I think, *But you don't listen to music much, and I also know you for an atheist or agnostic, so really, why would you want to come to a church and listen to organ music?* But I love you for wanting to be with me.

Another evening you accompany me to King Street East to an eclectic gathering of Corktown people, and after that, you never miss a Girls' Night Out — well, not when I host it, because you're not supposed to be there. It's girls only, and if you show up, other partners of the male persuasion will agitate to come, too.

Soon come treks to Oakville, Ontario. I announce that I'm going there to see the kids — my daughter, Helen, son-in-law, Jim, and granddaughters, Cameron and Rachel. Your eyes light up, and you've got that familiar little smile crinkling the corners of your mouth. You make it possible for me to take these frequent visits when you fly to Calgary to purchase your niece's Volkswagen Jetta. You do this for me, you who have no interest in cars and have rarely owned one. Recollections of that almost eighteen-hundred-mile drive across the Prairies and north of Lake Superior come to me when I remember the many phone calls you make describing it, and of your enormous pleasure hearing son Matt's plays broadcast on CBC Radio as you drive.

Each time I plan a visit to Oakville, you put away what you're working on and say you'll come, too. You might have a deadline. You really might not have the time, but you can't resist. And heaven help you, you even express interest in attending the girls' high school end-of-year concerts, which aren't always riveting. Piano recitals, as well.

There you are, patient, amused, often with that same slight smile. As your son, Matt, will later say, "My dad was basically a contented man."

• • •

After you've gone, long afterward, I'm lying across our bed in mid-afternoon deliberately summoning images of you, recalling memories of the time when you decide to take up skiing again — after how many years? We find out when you put your hand in the pocket of your old ski jacket and pull out a ski pass dated 1987. Really! Does a person forget how, or as on a bicycle, never forget? We're in that wooded, empty landscape of Upstate New York with Helen and Jim in their townhouse in Ellicottville they use for weekend skiing. Gathering at the foot of a hill, we watch you on your first try. Tall and athletic in your ski outfit, with an elegant parallel technique, you fly down the slope, only to fall into a crumpled heap at the bottom. But quickly your old skill returns and you ski advanced slopes. One day, you fall badly, and when eventually reaching the bottom of the hill, tell me you struck your head on a rock. Only later do you admit that it was sometime before you were able to get back on your skis, that you felt confused and wondered where you were and how you got there. A concussion, I think, but so much time has passed that it seems safe to assume there's been no intracranial or subdural bleeding.

My mind lingers in that picturesque little town, and I'm there with you in summer, in the memorial library, in coffee shops and restaurants. We're exploring the neighbouring countryside and its historic little towns, its lonely roads running through dense forest. Now we're wandering hand in hand through the arboretum, learning the names of all the trees, plants, and flowering bushes there. How interested and contented you are with everything we see and do. On late afternoons, we return to the house to read the books we purchased at a public library sale. One day, we even attempt to play tennis on the courts beyond the house. What a comedy! I haven't played in perhaps two decades, and my previous skill at wielding a racquet doesn't easily return.

I'm off again, rambling about in my mind, and next thing, we're up north in Magnetawan, in Burk's Falls, and in Bobcaygeon visiting your friend, Charles Pitcher. This little town on the Trent River has picturesque streets, a marina, a lock, and a river flowing through it, as well as a one-of-a-kind shopping experience of upscale women's clothes and shoes — considered a destination place for that reason.

I'm farther north now, making a long drive with you — six hours — north of North Bay to Cobalt for a two-week vacation, Matt coming with us for one of those weeks. You've long wanted to visit this cherished ancestral spot where family memories, legends, and tall tales flourish. We drive to Noranda where your family moved when you were six years old, where you walked alone to the local primary school. Sixty-plus years later, the two of us take that route, a twenty-minute trek that crosses railway tracks and a major highway. Most would consider it a tender age at which to begin the lessons of self-reliance and independence; modern parents would shudder, horrified and unable to relate.

That voyage down memory lane fills us with pleasure, and deep nostalgia for you. In one of the rare times you smile for the camera, you pose before a giant granite rock that rises in the middle of the playground, and again, in front of the house that was yours for a brief two years. A wooden structure with green window sashes, it sits on a corner lot that edges Noranda's downtown. Again, we walk that route to the school and back, marvelling at risks that at the time weren't considered as such, at the endurance of one small child.

14

You Can Do Anything

All of this activity, all this travelling, is interspersed with family functions: birthday celebrations, Easter and Thanksgiving dinners, Christmas, and others.

Next, we're on a sailing boat with your friend, Al Workman, on

Lake Ontario. It's only then that I learn you can sail. Next, I discover you can fly, that you even have a pilot's licence!

I only hear about this now. The question returns: how well can one person ever know another?

"Sweetie, is there anything you can't do?" I ask.

"Well, I did what I thought was impossible and married you."

"I think you've said that before …"

15

A Literary Adventure

Today, in my memory, again I see you standing in the doorway to my office, leaning against the door frame. I've asked you to analyze a synopsis of my novel *Helena: An Odyssey*. You shift your posture. Alertness comes over you much like a cat suddenly becoming intensely aware of its surroundings. From my desk chair, I glance up, and up at you — what an arresting sight! I've written many drafts of my novel's summary and can no longer see clearly through my forest of words. You scrutinize what I've written and give me suggestions. I scribble down the words as they come out of your mouth, and next thing, I've got a riveting synopsis.

Thank you, Gordon!

Helena: An Odyssey is my first novel after three books of non-fiction published over the past dozen-plus years. Researching and writing this tome has consumed me for many years and become my outsize ambition. Almost unknown to me has been the history of Greeks living in Turkey over the centuries, the catastrophe that befell them after the First World War, and the war between Greeks and Turks that ensued. The forebearers of Kiki, my hairdresser, were among the victims of those displaced. Inspired to write the history in fictional form and make it better known became an absorbing, multi-year passion, continuing to grow in scope until my original two-generational family expanded to three, then four, even five generations.

How you encourage me. You listen to me but never read the various drafts. This puzzles and disappoints me. Then, one night in bed when the book is in its final draft, I see you so captivated reading something on your Kindle that I ask you what it is.

"*Helena: An Odyssey.*" You glance over at me, eyes twinkling. A pause, then you add, "I love it!"

Without my knowing, you've uploaded it.

"I didn't want to read it until it was in its final draft," you explain.

I think about this, remembering that long ago I learned you're incapable of being insincere, that if you didn't really approve and like the novel, stubbornly you would have refused to make any comment.

· · ·

It's 2015, and we begin planning a book launch. You're there, directing all your time and energy to help me organize an ambitious event at Mr. Greek Restaurant on Danforth Avenue. You invite all your colleagues, and I, everyone I know. But still I fret. "It's such a huge space. How can I possibly fill it?"

Danforth is arguably one of the most popular streets in Toronto, and Mr. Greek, one of the largest and most flamboyant restaurants anywhere, is owned by my hairdresser Kiki's sister and brother-in-law. We're there early and watch, dumbfounded, as people come in their dozens, and more dozens, until the place is filled and spilling over. The food, wine, and beer — all of it is spectacular, and the hum of conversation never ceases. My speech includes why I was motivated to write about the war between the Greeks and Turks, about the cruel forced exchange of populations, the burning of Smyrna (now called Izmir), about a refugee family forced into a poor part of Greece and their subsequent journey to Toronto. Over all the generations, the burden of reclaiming family wealth and reputation hangs heavily. My hairdresser was, and is, my heroine, and I've modelled my fictional heroine on her.

Afterward, when I've sold all my books, keeping but one, when the crowds have gone and you and I gather up our stuff, a young Turkish woman enters, sees the cover of my remaining book, and immediately wants to buy it. "It's also the story of the Turks," she says. "You should write my story — as a Turk."

I know you're very proud of me, Gordon. But you never say so, not perhaps until many months later when finding the courage, you voice the words in the way you did after a talk I gave at a large library, in the way you did long after a Christmas dinner given by the president of a mining company when I ribbed him, he an Aussie and I, a Kiwi, about our friendly rivalry. You say long after, "I was very proud of you." I understand how difficult it is for you to say words that express your emotions. But also, how difficult or impossible for you to lie, even to prevaricate as would seem kind after those times I delivered talks that didn't go particularly well. I know it, and afterward, looking for reassurance, even just to discuss it, I ask you what you think. You remain silent, not one word offered to soften my own self-judgment. While disappointed, I admire your integrity, that you won't offer false reassurance, even for me.

As British novelist Sarah Dunant has written, "If you love a man for his honesty, you cannot become angry when he shows it."

16

To See the World

We're back to wanting to travel, particularly to exotic places and cultures — nowhere is off limits.

At first, you say, "Let's go to Iran."

"How about Russia?"

And together in what now feels like the very few years we have, at various times we walk all over Manhattan and parts of Brooklyn. We wander around regions of Italy and spend a month in London. We ride the railways that run all over Britain. Then, on public buses, we criss-cross Turkey, Greece, spend time in Florence, Portugal, and Mexico. One winter, we drive to Florida. And somehow in between we make several visits to New Zealand.

Not least, we sightsee all over Toronto as though we don't know our own city. Particular joys include pastry shops within walking distance of bookshops. Picking up friends or relatives from the airport but first heading to a Coffee Time to indulge in apple fritters or cinnamon buns while watching planes fly low overhead. Simple joys but multiplied many times by our shared love of them.

I'm remembering your travels throughout Asia, and now regret that I didn't ask you more about those experiences. Why? I suppose now that I wanted to live in the moment. Each of us had a long history, we were young in our relationship, and it was the present, the future, that mattered.

17

A Side Trip to Hospital

At some point in our beautiful lives, I experience two episodes of sudden illness in the form of a rapidly spreading cellulitis up my right arm, neck, and face, accompanied by a high fever. Its onset was a cut finger. The first time, I feel very ill and lie prostrate in bed with a high fever that persists for two days. When eventually I get up, it's to see an ugly red rash dancing up my arm, neck, and the side of my face. After my right ear begins bleeding, it occurs to me that I should get medical help. My vulnerability to such infections stems from a chronic autoimmune disease for which I'm treated every eight weeks with immune-suppressant drugs called biologicals. This has never presented me with a problem or any limitations — until now.

You sit at my bedside by day and many nights until I'm discharged. Thank you, Gordon!

Afterward, our lives continue in ever-changing patterns — is there such a thing? I'll jump up on a Saturday morning, but only after you've read through the entire *Globe and Mail*.

I hover about you.

"Do I need to do something?" you ask.

"Yes, we should make plans to go travelling again."

"Where to?"

"I think I suggested Russia before I got sick. Your turn. Where would you like to go?"

"Iran."

"You said that before."

"Yes, and I've got a contact there who can arrange a small group of us."

"You said that before, too."

But we both know there's not much chance of this, so we consider other destinations, both of us preferring exotic places and cultures to the familiar. Nowhere is off limits.

• • •

We travel, not to Russia, not to Iran, but to Greece. Much later, as I search my collections of photos online, I smile and weep over them, since they're both a consolation and a torment. Images come to me of the many beds we made love in, slept in, and dreamed in during our exotic travels. Twin beds. King beds. Tiny loft beds under mosquito nets, at night, the two of us becoming one. And so, through the photos I embark on our earliest travels, trips we couldn't wait to take together, this time to Greece, you suggesting we check out cities and the landscape where I set *Helena*.

Next, we're in Athens! We walk it early and late, in and out of markets of every kind filled with objects of every kind. We're seduced into purchasing two watercolour paintings, both with quintessential Greek scenes. The one that captures your eye features an old Greek man bent over a newspaper.

"It could be you with ten years added," I say, delighted, not knowing that another ten years isn't what you will get. Athens: we trek to art galleries and museums. We sit on a curb to watch a strike unfolding, one that spins into a huge, riotous public party with music, food, balloons, costumes. "Only the Greeks!" I say, laughing.

It's in Athens where you have your wallet stolen after a train journey from the Port of Piraeus. We travelled north from the Peloponnesus and stopped briefly at this famous, ancient deep-sea port that I wished we had more time to explore, since it's a place that's existed in various forms since the sixth century BCE. In the railway carriage opposite us are two men we later figure are Bulgarians. Each stares hard at us for the entire trip. Having to exit the train early because of a blockage at the next station, everyone heads for the escalator. One of the two men goes down first, the other remains at the top. The man at the bottom doesn't step off, and everyone above him falls onto the one below. In the ensuing chaos, the man above reaches into your front trouser pocket and removes your wallet — a well-orchestrated robbery. How you swear, then horrified, you turn to me and say, "I'm so sorry for swearing in front of you."

"Well, I've heard those words before." Despite the catastrophe, I smile. But you're humiliated, since you've travelled extensively all your life without such mishap. On the street level, I notice a sign proclaiming a hotel called Caroline.

"Hey, a good omen," I say, and there we remain for a few days until you receive temporary travel documents. The silver lining is that it gives us more time to explore Athens.

Then follows a terrifying train journey north to Thessaloniki where we're to stay with a friend's brother. The track tilts on the very edge of precipitous cliffs that drop into ravines many hundreds of feet below us. What a landscape!

Dimitri's house, Mediterranean in style, is surrounded by olive groves and sits on a slope above the city. Dimitri, a gentle man, a scholar, is a history professor at the University of Thessaloniki. Through him, and through our own exploring, we become acquainted with this city's tumultuous history, but our first impressions are of a place relaxing tranquilly on the shores of the Aegean Sea in a manner that suggests it's finished with its violent past. Images collide in my memory: once a Roman, then a Byzantine, then an Ottoman city, now a modern-day Greek one, it offers apologies for its past in the form of a large sculpture that suggests to me broken arms and legs in a tangled and tortured mass that represents the fifty-five thousand Jews killed in that city.

We spend one evening on the beach watching costumed folk dancing that is as old as the land itself.

One morning, we check out the museum in the White Tower on the waterfront, a structure that was once a twelfth-century Byzantine fortification, then a notorious prison and the scene of mass executions during Ottoman rule. Now, under Greek control, it's been remodelled and whitewashed, hence the name White Tower.

Dimitri takes us to Anopolis on the upper slopes of Thessaloniki to a tiny chapel beside a triple wall built in ancient Byzantine and Turkish times. We stand in its entranceway where it's believed St. Paul the Apostle once stood to preach his First Epistle to the Thessalonians. On learning this, I feel a huge surge of emotion, sense myself walking backward into history, into another reality. I gaze at you and wonder what you're thinking. Religion, personal beliefs — we rarely talk about them. Picking up lit candles, we enter the dim interior of the chapel to find little else other than an altar and candles burning.

Back in the chapel's entranceway, we scan the hill sloping away below us, and in the dim light of early evening, we can all but discern the ghosts of those long-ago people gathered in groups listening to the new epistle being preached two thousand years ago. Standing where St. Paul positioned himself, we listen for his voice ringing out over those hills, preaching about the glory of God and the need for repentance. Whether believers or not, we're deeply moved.

Afterward, in the valley below, we stroll over a patch of ground punctuated by hillocks and small bridges — an agora where it's believed St. Symeon, a Thessalonian monk, bishop, and theologian, walked six hundred years earlier.

Leaving Thessaloniki, we journey south to the Gulf of Corinth, a place where history and mythology meet, and where, if we could but stay a while, we would have visited the Temple of Aphrodite.

I look at you at the edge of the canal examining large ships edging toward it, watch you take photos. We're touching history, here in this famous gulf that separates the Peloponnese from western mainland Greece, a place where, in 873 CE, a battle was fought between the Byzantine Empire and the Cretan Saracens.

Again, I feel the presence of St. Paul, even if he probably didn't actually visit this place, something that still remains unknown. But he did write epistles to these early Corinthian Christians around 53–54 CE, letters illuminating his thoughts about the problems of the early church, about immorality, marriage, celibacy, the conduct of women, the impropriety of eating meat offered to idols. Not the least, about the worthy reception of the Eucharist.

Sadly, we've got no time to stop at Delphi, only to meander about the canal, to cross it, and be met by my hairdresser's sister, Joanna, who drives us for several hours to the old Roman port city of Patras on the west coast of the Peloponnese.

18

Patras

My urgency to get to this western city sharpens because this is what I've come to Greece for: to peer into those places I feel I already know, where sometimes I think I've already lived, the scenes I used for *Helena*. I remember how driven I'd been to tell the little-known story about Greeks and Turks and the war between them in 1920–22. Now I can't wait to enter those places, that city, the little refugee street I believe I already know, as though I've already lived there.

But first, you, I, and Joanna roam Patras's old, cobbled streets and the buildings above them that lean crookedly into one another. We climb the steps to its upper level where grandiose homes with spectacular views stare over the Ionian Sea. Returning to its teeming lower level, we saunter around Georgiou Square to watch the life of the local people. In the afternoon, we explore old Roman ruins.

I learn that Patras is the largest city in the Peloponnese and is the western gateway to Greece. A lively city of shops, tavernas, and cafés, it also has one of the biggest universities in the country. You, Gordon, never tire of taking photos of it, and of me against a background of ancient buildings, against statues in Georgiou Square, and the backdrop of the Cathedral of Saint Andrew, one of the largest in Europe.

At last we move on to the old refugee street where I set *Helena*. I've written about this street, peopled it with fictional characters, and dreamed about it. I can now check out its current reality. For me, it's with both joy and an aching heart that I head with you and Joanna to that scrubby little street.

Joanna seems to have dropped angel-like, into our lives, to land on a place and among people that promise wonders beyond those of the everyday. In appearance and personality, she's the incarnation of Kiki, my hairdresser in Toronto. A perpetual smile lights up her broad, suntanned face, a hint of mischief lurking in her wide brown eyes. She drives us to the outskirts of the city to a narrow street that spills across the railway lines in bits and pieces. It goes nowhere, only to a stony pathway that leads to the beach and the green Ionian Sea.

We park at the end of the overgrown and largely abandoned street. For a moment, I wonder if you'll be bored, because this is my story, my passion, and my many years' work. I glance at you sideways to see you enjoying this, notice that familiar little smile crinkling the corners of your mouth, your eyes dancing. How I love you! How little I know about you!

At last I'm in a place I've so long dreamed about, have imagined, and can immediately grasp the way it once must have been — a line of ugly little houses, shapeless women wandering it. It's then Eleni, one of my tragic heroines, comes to me. She leans against the door frame of her tiny house in a posture telling me that every bone in her body aches at the immensity of what she's lost, descended from Greeks who for centuries in Turkey lived harmoniously among Turks, Jews, and Muslims, then cast out with nothing, abandoned in this desolate place. She's come full circle, back to her beginnings: a shack with a dirt floor, no toilet, only squatting knees to chin over an open toilet. No running water, no cooking facilities. And poor Spiros, her brother-in-law: perhaps this misshapen brother of my character, Adam, has suffered the more. I conjure him sitting on a plank before a ramshackle table down near the docks, hawking his miserable wares until he's hoarse. But having lived without routine, he's learned of its pleasures. When rain and wind beats at him, he prizes the knowledge that he has somewhere to go each day, each one born in the hope of something better.

My emotions run high as Joanna's cousin, Angeliki, takes us to the long-abandoned family home, gesticulating while talking volubly in Greek. We can only nod and smile and smile some more.

These Greek refugees worked, suffered, and grieved, but eventually coalesced into a warm and lively community in this narrow street where we now walk. Its silence shrieks at us, its history written in abandoned communal kitchens, a rusted public tap, a stony path that goes nowhere. I feel it. I can see those refugees, hear their wails, their shrieks of despair, but also their murmurs of hope.

As we leave, Angeliki smiles at you, Gordon, then stretches out a hand and offers a rosary. It's a gift to someone she feels is special, though she scarcely knows you. She's like so many others, like small children, like small and large dogs and cats attracted to you who creep to your side, intuitively knowing they'll be safe, accepted, non-judged, and welcomed.

19

A Bedtime Obsession

It's a warm September day, and I'm up on the third floor, imagining you at your standing desk, remembering all the time you spent there. I sit in your empty chair and look for you as though you're hiding somewhere, fix my eyes on that desk and will your silhouette to take form, for my vision of you to become real. You're in your pajama pants, socks, the black jacket you wore all winter over a T-shirt. Your curly white hair is tossed about just the way I like it. How often did I run my hands through it to mess it up the way it was when you emerged from bed, out of the shower? On the railing hang pajama pants and shorts, sneakers below, a headband and water bottle on a shelf beside the elliptical machine — how seriously you took this exercise!

One day, I take Rumi's poems and some of the poet Hafiz's up to that third floor to sit in your chair and read them. I feel they're giving me permission to mourn and weep, particularly when something unexpected, even trivial, hits me and I absorb anew the enormity of what I've lost. I call you to mind every waking second, remember your face, the beautiful form of you, all the big and little things we did. I sound like a jilted lover pleading with an errant husband: "Please come back! Why are you staying away so long? I'm so sorry for anything I did that you didn't like."

Why am I sorry? What did I suppose you didn't like? Well, for the questions I didn't ask about your life, the times I didn't show more curiosity about your early years travelling. For any time I overrode your wishes after you expressed them. It's hard to tell the truth about ourselves, I suppose, because we're afraid we'll be defined by our worst decisions instead of our best — I know!

I go downstairs, through the long corridor into the dining room, and then the kitchen. Your photos are all around the walls, and there you are, looking out at me, smiling, thoughtful — joyful as in the wedding photos. How can I bear the loss of you? I return again and again to those photos and am simultaneously comforted and devastated at my loss. Each evening, I take a sheaf of photos of you and gaze at each one in turn, my bedtime obsession.

20

What Do We Owe the Dead?

What do we owe the dead? To celebrate their birthdays? Read the books they read? (I try!) Prepare the food they liked? Wear the clothes they wore? What does it mean to do so? Perhaps if I wear your shirt or your jacket, Gordon, I'll feel myself closer to you, will remember you more vividly, more immediately, pretend you're still here. You wear mostly blue, which so suits you, blue the colour of sea and sky, of blue jay wings, forget-me-nots, and bluebells. How I love the bottomlessness of your deep-set eyes.

Again, I remember how much you liked to read and try to do justice to your science magazines. A news junkie, a science junkie, you absorbed knowledge from newspapers, professional journals, *Scientific American*, books about Russian history, about calculus, about the universe in numbers, about randomness in life and the origins of the universe. And then you come to my book club to read novels. The joy of you surrounds me. I listen for comments others make about you — *modest* being the word I most often hear.

"Gordon has very interesting ideas and often a different slant on things," someone says. "He's truly erudite but doesn't present as such."

"Gordon has an interesting face," Max Miller, a portrait painter in Bobcaygeon comments. "High cheekbones and a beautifully sculpted jaw. He has an ethereal air about him, like one foot in the physical realm and the other in a spiritual realm. He might be engaging with you, but he's also somewhere else in his mind."

"Gordon was very easygoing and comfortable to be with," says his colleague, Joe Hinzer. "He had different and very interesting views on all subjects."

I know you for being a don't-look-at-me kind of person, valuing objects, experiences, and knowledge for themselves and not necessarily with a desire to share what you know with others. To most of us, you were a sort of King Solomon — I think I've called you that before — wise, judicious, thoughtful, a problem solver, the go-to person for just about everything. It sounds as if I'm building you up to near-mythical proportions and am in danger of creating a saint. Of course, you weren't — thank God! But what a mix. You fill up a place with a large presence, wherever that place is. You are the half of the two of us with all the wisdom, humour, knowledge, and when with you, I feel taller, more interesting, more fun, more important.

One day, I walk to the home of my Corktown friends, Vanessa and Francine, and involve myself in conversations, in jokes. But simmering beneath my surface calm lies an undercurrent of sadness that often threatens to undo me. Briefly, we talk about gardens and where best to grow rose of Sharon bushes. Gardens: it comes to me that everything I engage in is for the two of us, like gardening. I manicure ours, back and front, plant, weed, and sweep the paths. Right now, I drop out of the conversation because another image jumps up — my latest trip to the local flower nursery. I returned with plants and are digging when you come upon me. Your eyes are smiling, your voice indulgent, as you ask, "Did you buy out the whole nursery?"

"No, but come and look at this." And proudly I show you the recently swept walkways, the trimmed bushes, the new plantings of flowers. Now, the sight of the garden reproaches me with its vacant look, empty, though it's not, only in a ghostly way. Empty of you, Gordon, for you sat long under the sun there, reading. Returning from this recent social visit, I walk up Berkeley Street from Dundas, which I've done a thousand times, only on this occasion the street feels empty, faded. I've been here long ago in some other life. "I'm done with this street," I say aloud, then feel horrified. "But I love it! Where will I go?"

What a rich household we had. We filled it up with ourselves and our love, and with two perfect cats that somewhere along the way we inherited from my son and family. How you enjoy them. How amused you are when you say around ten every night, "Come on, boys, time for your treats." And you head toward the basement where they're to sleep for the night. Anticipating what they're about to receive, both run downstairs and wait, each in a particular spot, knowing exactly where you'll place their treats.

And so over shapeless days and weeks and months, I console myself with memories. I summon images of you: the way you walked — leisurely, totally unhurried, even while crossing a street in front of oncoming traffic — until the day our garage door is about to come down on you and you have to sprint to get out from under it. How I laughed! Sometimes, when you go out on errands, go shopping, to an appointment, I run to the front window to watch as you walk up the street. Unknown to you, I admire the beauty of your physical frame, your loping stride, the shy angle of your head.

Is this how life is? That we're always waiting, dreaming, running about, hoping for something up ahead, then suddenly one day, find out this indeed *is* our life.

With your death, my darling, what is my life to be?

21
The Empty Door

Alone in the house for two days of writing, I feel the need to get out, to do something. All the while, the world stretches before me dry, sterile. I go to Staples to buy file folders, then to Loblaws at Queen's Quay. I've taken a book with me and sit upstairs to read it while having coffee. The windows overlook the lake and a sugar refinery. Afterward, as I walk in the parking lot toward my/our car, again that smothering sadness falls over me.

"I'm so tired of having no one to talk to," I tell you. "No one to do things for — like all this shopping. Why don't you come home? Why have you been away so long?" This is my plaintive cry. I'm remembering all this, and every day that passes, again in my mind, you assume an immensity that fills the house, the streets, the libraries, the shops, until you're everywhere. There's not a moment when you don't entirely fill up my thoughts: I see you on dusty streets, sprawled in the sunroom armchair, stretched out on your side of the bed with a book or magazine in your hands. I watch you coming out of the shower, hear you on the stairs. Then suddenly, when I catch sight of you through an open doorway, the poem about the empty door repeats itself ceaselessly in my brain.

The empty door. I will meet you at the empty door. Enter the atrium that held our dreams once bold — oh, yes, we dreamed big dreams, intimate, joyful ones. *Now I live with regrets untold* — how can it be otherwise? We felt we were on the cusp of a shimmering future that stretched to infinity, one we fashioned exactly how we wanted it. Intoxicated with our love and the unfolding of our lives, we turned to each other and said, "So when should we start our family, you know, have kids?"

"I think we talked about this ..."

"But we didn't actually decide on how many."

Yes, I've *walked corridors of restlessness, bathed in pools of forgetfulness*. But not yet for me is there the fraying of life, because I have things to do, among them, embark on a journey to understand those enigmatic parts of you that eluded me during our life together, you, this almost unknowable man I married. Your son, Matt, too.

22

The Empty Chair

If you are anywhere, you'll see that I write to you every night. I'm making a book for you and will call it *Looking for Gordon*, with a subtitle *The Shape of Love*.

I'm back to *the empty chair* — here it is again, always in my subconscious — the chair where you sat when not at your stand-up desk working, reading, sorting our finances. I know when you're tired because I hear a crash as you collapse into it, that chair where I found you with your familiar shape filling it. But you'd left me already. Now, as though on a pilgrimage to get to know more about you, I walk upstairs to that empty chair, sit in it, talk to you. I glimpse you at your desk, feel your presence when I look around at all your accumulated stuff: the eye charts, the rock collections, and the whole paraphernalia of a busy working office.

Now, I'm back on the matrimonial bed, once more intensely searching my mind for clues to your elusive personality.

Your brother, Murray, comments that rarely did you share your thoughts, ambitions, desires, and when returning from travelling for three to four years in Asia, you tell him you've always wanted to do just this — to travel for the sake of it — but he doesn't remember your ever mentioning it.

But you freely express yourself in your birthday, Christmas, and Mother's Day cards to me. Criticism I never hear you give. In the beginning, I suppose your world was small. I remember your telling me what your mother once said: "You'll never be disappointed, Gordon, because you don't expect much from life." I don't know at what point she said this and wonder now if it was as simple statement of fact as she saw it, or the expression of disappointment on your behalf, maybe a warning, perhaps reassurance? You, a man without an ego. A modest man. A non-hierarchical man. You seem to have little need for love, for approval or recognition. But surely all people need some, and I see how you absorb everything I give you.

23

Everyone Inherits Something

In those early courting days — but did we know then we were courting? — we are about to go to a local political meeting. I wait for you outside your open condo door. An old sewing machine stands just inside, acting as a hall table of sorts. Beyond the short hallway, all I can see are dustballs and one lace-up shoe on its side. I wonder where the other is. The day you invite me in, after seeing the chaos of your physical surroundings, I look at you. You're not at all embarrassed; you're even oblivious to what I see. Upstairs is one bedroom, but perhaps there were two and you removed a wall. Where the second bed might have been stands an exercise bicycle, the hook at the back loaded with clothes. Business cards are scattered about the floor along with dustballs. I absorb all this with amusement. That evening, you set up a projector and screen and play movies of your childhood in Cobalt. There's only one large chair, so we sit in it together — perhaps our first moments of intimacy.

That comment of your mother's about your not being disappointed in life because you don't expect much keeps returning to me. It's clear to me you had no need to show to anyone what or who you are. Did you learn at a young age to mask your essential core? Except, of course, for your views on public affairs and science. If so, it must have become a habit.

This prompts me to ask: Is it possible to resist the iron engine of one's childhood? An engine that according to many, drives you forward until the day you die. Again to many, a man might have a wife/husband and kids, but the new family is ghostly compared to the old. But is it? As the novelist George Eliot once wrote: "For there is no creature whose inward being is so strong that it is not greatly determined by what lies outside it" — a statement sure to create controversy.

I've been speaking again to your brother, Murray, just one year younger, asking him about you when you were young and growing up together, going to university, and how it was when you both attended St. Michael's College. Murray tells me that after the first year, students were separated according to ability, the brightest into the Brain Class. You, Gordon — of course! — were entered into this one, with Murray after you. You excelled in all subjects, including Latin and German.

"Gordon loved mathematics above everything," Murray tells me. Yes, there's a colossal tome on your desk entitled *A History of the Universe in Numbers*. "At university, and probably influenced by our dad, he changed from geology to civil engineering, and finally to mining engineering."

As I say elsewhere, you weren't contented with mining, not enjoying it, so you obtained a degree in computer science at Humber College. This, I think, you were born to do. Your sister, Mimi, says that like your father, who seemed to have intuitive knowledge of where to find iron ore bodies, so you had a similar sense of the pathways of coding. Also, like your father, like many of your siblings, you were driven by an entrepreneurial spirit.

So everyone inherits something. None of us walks away unburdened.

"He forced us to sleep in a tent outside in midwinter," Murray says of your father. "He wanted to toughen us up — well, Gordon mostly. He sent us out to the hockey rink without hats, mittens, scarves. 'Get your brother outside,' he would repeat. 'Get him on the rink.' Gordon didn't mind playing street hockey or soccer with local kids, but mostly he wanted to curl up with a book, with science magazines and newspapers."

I know, Gordon, you experienced rejection for the longest time from your father, though in the end he became proud of you.

Your childhood. Your adulthood. My life after you — or did I suppose it already to be over? — my life that has to begin again without you, a journey where I try to learn more about you after you're gone. Like a needle stuck on a vinyl disc, I return again and again to what I know of your formative years when you were only eight years old attending public school in Noranda, to you as a little boy.

You told me before how your father came upon you reading, roared at you, told you your brains would fry and your eyes fall out if you didn't stop. Reading: your joy and passion in life — well, until you met me and I became your very great love, your joy, and your passion being to love me. What conceit! How do I know this so absolutely when I've described you as having difficulty expressing your feelings to any other?

I've felt it. I've known it without your using words of love, which eventually you do. Everyone who sees us knows it.

I've memorized the inscriptions in those cards for birthdays, Christmas, Mother's Day that tell me of your love. On a card smothered in roses:

> For my wife, Carolyn: I love you more than all the roses in the world.
> Carolyn: you make my heart sing. You are my everything.
> Carolyn, my beloved, I love you forever and ever and ever.
> Carolyn: you are the best wife in the world.

For you, it was safer to write than to speak of love.

But how, in the end, can one ever really know another? You would often disappear in your mind and stare far beyond the people and places around you. So where were you? You're not a storyteller and so not easily able to explain your thoughts or describe your travels. I suppose I do know you and so don't ask the questions about things I now so much want to know, like your young dreams, your visions for your life, about your travels.

24

Looking for You

I'm in the sunroom, Gordon, looking at the empty chair beside me and am suddenly seized with a desire to talk to one of your siblings, to talk about you. David is closest, so I phone and ask if he has any spare moments could he drop over sometime. He comes, always faithful to his brother's memory, and to me. I ask him what he can remember about your early life, even though he's seventeen and half years younger.

In his typical understated manner, he tells me the fragments he recalls, among other things, how both you and Murray dated good-looking girls when young.

"So what happened?" I ask. "Did Gordon — or the girl — give up after one date?"

David has no answer. If it was the girl, little did she know what she was missing!

With David gone, I feel drab, depleted. I get up and peer in the mirror to see a little old lady, bleakness in her eyes, though she tries hard to conceal it. But the day will come when this old woman will fade into dust and into a nondescript, indecipherable landscape. Who will remember her and her beloved Gordon? They loved each other, yes; she makes sure the world knows this. She'll remember him, turn him into a saint, the ideal man, husband and friend — well, she already did that during his life. And she'll hang on to this vision because this is now her identity, one she'll use to gain attention or sympathy or some special status for herself if lacking others, for after all, who retains any importance when getting old — older — important only to themselves as they walk into a bitter twilight?

Gordon, when you met me, had you grown tired of living in the world alone? What made you notice me?

Oh, that's a story in itself, one even I can't find some of the details of how you and I came about. I do remember when you look at me with eyes liquid blue and shimmering, like that time in Toronto's

Flatiron Building in the Down Under Pub on Front Street where we have drinks.

We decide to check it out. Just another pub, really, but one whose building has a history, and we both love history! So I research the Flatiron for us.

"Once this property had a building called the Coffin Block," I tell you. "Then the Gooderham distillery family bought the land in the 1890s, tore down the Coffin Block, and replaced it with the Flatiron, using it as their offices. How I love its Romanesque Revival cornice, the frieze above the arched windows."

I don't know how much time passed or how much we drank before I say, "Hey, let's go. We've got other things to do." You know what I have in mind, and there it is again — that warm, shy expression in your eyes.

Another day, I procure tickets for us to a private art gallery opening in Yorkville, then to high tea in the Four Seasons Hotel. Sitting opposite each other in conversation, again I say, "Let's go. We've got other things to do."

I can write about you now, my darling, words that have colour, texture, an aroma. I can create phrases that sing, that light up the universe. I write them, but they don't stick on the page, on the screen. They're just words without substance, nothing solid on which to hang them — only sometimes when I think and write about our travels, and when I write about much more, of course. But a big part of our lives, I realize, *was* our travelling. How many times to Britain? I must go there in my mind again soon, try to rescue myself after my recent despondent mood.

But I remain lying across our bed's white counterpane, inert. How many months have passed? I count them, perturbed that I still weep almost every evening for you, and sometimes during the day. I get up and return to my laptop, to the photos. This time, nine months later, I click on the ones taken in New Zealand.

New Zealand: I remember how much I wanted to show you all of this gorgeous country. And to show off you, my husband.

"This is my husband." I say this whenever an opportunity presents itself. Whenever I look at you, I feel lifted up, a sort of exultation that

I should have been so lucky to have found you. Actually, though, I think it might have been you who found me.

Wherever we go in New Zealand, whether it's to a subtropical island called Waiheke or to far-flung Gisborne on the east coast, a road trip around South Island, then back to Waiheke in a tiny, mosquito-ridden shack in the bush, I see how you absorb it all and embrace it, and I love you for that.

Another day, or a week, maybe a month passes, and I'm back searching the photos. What am I looking for? Just more snaps of you. I run through them on my laptop until my eyes are sore and I have to turn away. But such is my urgency to revisit our life together and especially the beginnings that I keep coming back to them, searching for something I haven't yet identified.

I phone your friends and colleagues. "Tell me about Gordon and what he did," I beg. I feel stupid because someone might say to me, "You're only asking now? Why didn't you find out from Gordon when he was alive?"

One colleague of yours has dementia and can't remember much. However, Bob Stobie, your good friend, tells me he was in awe of your intelligence and abilities. "I wouldn't have described Gordon as particularly extroverted," Bob says, "but he was very good at making technical presentations, particularly to potential customers. His ability to speak a fair bit of French paid off," he adds. "One year in the middle of the tax season, he was uncertain about a detail for a corporate tax return and figured out the name of the person that he wished to speak to. [Good luck trying to get English-language information.] He got through immediately with the French number."

Charles Pitcher clues me in to much of what you shared with him. You took me up to meet him at his mansion in Bobcaygeon on the Trent River and the marina he owns. I've since returned to have a week's vacation with him. We talk about you. Charles, as CEO of Western Canadian Coal in Vancouver, hired you as a consultant, not once but twice.

What you did for him was this: when a property or an enterprise, usually a large mining corporation, was put up for sale, you evaluated it for the benefit of the potential buyer, typically another corporation.

You placed a value on the production costs, the potential sales, its likely profitability, the state of world markets, its possible future. Mathematical — yes, indeed.

25

The Peloponnese

During one of those interminable evenings when time refuses to move, after many days when I go to bed early, get up late, days when I have no hunger, no thirst, no dreams or memories, eventually I prod myself to do something — to write! I remember I've left us in the middle of my historical novel *Helena* in Patras. I say to you, "I know you like travelling, but how much is enough? Joanna wants us to take us to her home in the eastern Peloponnese for a day or two. What do you think?"

Your expression says, *How can you even ask me?*

Next, in my mind, we're driving with Joanna right across southern Greece into the eastern mountains in the province of Ermionida. Sweeping vistas fall away on both sides — hills and valleys, little human habitation, the iridescent blue of the Aegean Sea glimpsed over every dip in sunlit hills, sprawling fish farms here and there.

High in the hills are further panoramas, endless spreading vistas glimpsed from dusty, twisting roads, then suddenly we stop before a mansion — no, a castle — rising right there at the roadside, looming out of the early evening as though having just been planted.

Joanna leaps from the driver's seat and points to this mansion before us, perhaps a castle? We step from the roadside onto the bottom step of a pub with a large restaurant behind.

Up marble steps, a second floor, a third, which is to be our living quarters: two bedrooms, an elongated living space, two bathrooms. Spectacular views. All this is to be ours. I'm in fairyland! In the restaurant that evening, Joanna guides us to a table in a corner. My impressions are of spacious, airy rooms close to the roadside, one leading to another and another; of many courses of Greek food created by Joanna's husband, Yannis; of Joanna, a queen, a diva who sings arias as she moves across the cavernous space that is her home and empire, surely a goddess in a golden temple set in an ancient land. Or I, dreaming, have been transported into some magical realm brushed by angel wings.

We're joined by a British couple who come to dine in the restaurant every year.

"When you're not busy, will you join us?" I ask Joanna as she floats by our table. She does. And in this enchanted setting, in this fairy-tale castle, we talk of love.

"We've been married fifty-four years," the British couple tell us, waiting to hear what we'll reveal about ourselves.

"This is really our honeymoon," I answer, laughing at their surprise, the questions on their lips they don't like to ask. Then, because we've been talking about love, I tell the story of Kiki and Joanna's father, who while he was married to the most beautiful woman in Patras had many affairs. When confronted by his wife, he said, "I see lots of women cold and hungry and they got no one to love them. I tell you, no woman should get to be without love. So I love them."

We all stare at one another, both moved and scandalized.

"But, Joanna," I eventually say, "I know from your sister that your father was also a man who loved his wife, loved his children fiercely and absolutely."

Ah, so really in the end, he was faithful, but in his own way. Fidelity, or lack of it, to a person or an idea is the subject of so many stories told in fiction and poetry. You, Gordon, asked nothing of me other than that I love you. And as surely as the moon dictates the tides, as the sun crosses the sky, you know that I do, that I'll be faithful to you and you to me until the end of time. And how soon that time comes!

On the rooftop the next morning, we gaze over a largely empty, primordial landscape where only goat paths punctuate pristine hills and valleys. In the distance, illuminated by the rising sun, we glimpse a lonely goatherder leading his flock.

"They poison our dogs," Joanna says as she places before us bowls of homemade yogurt with honey poured into it.

"Divine!" I exclaim as I dip my spoon into the gleaming white mass. "What do you mean, they poison your dogs?"

"We live among very poor people," she answers. "They're jealous of what we have and want to take it away. They say that because we're rich we should serve them in the restaurant for free."

I shiver as images come of people still living the way of life of distant forebears who, envious, seek to destroy those who have more than they do, who threaten the introduction of newer ways of living.

26

New Zealand Again

You never tire of going to New Zealand, Gordon, but then, you never get weary of travelling. I see in you the desire to see, grasp, understand, and perhaps go where no one else has been. We make yet another trip there, this time to drive around the entire South Island, down the west coast, along the south, and up the east to Nelson. Another honeymoon, but then our whole lives together have been one long, blissful honeymoon.

A train ride through King Country brings us to the very heart of North Island. King Country, so named after the Māori king Tawhiao. Low mountain ranges here. River valleys. Headwaters of the Mangatutu, Waipa, Mangaokewa, Ongarue. Volcanic peaks known as the Three Sisters soar: Tongariro at over six thousand feet, Ngauruhoe with more than seven, Ruapehu with nine thousand. Tongariro National Park is also in this region.

We cross Cook Strait to Picton, a picturesque major transport hub near a small town dotted with phoenix palm trees. It's also the place where short-story writer Katherine Mansfield spent time with her grandparents.

On that first day, we rent a car and drive to Nelson. This beautiful little city is the geographic centre of New Zealand, and for reasons not known to me as I write this, I feel very emotional thinking about our brief time there. Perhaps because this is the beginning of what I think of as our South Island odyssey, our idyll. Maybe also because I'm proudly showing you what is mine, this new young land of my forebears. I see again Nelson's wide streets dotted with coffee shops and restaurants, its flowering shrubs and distant hills. Nothing particularly memorable occurs to create the vividness of my memories, but they pop out at me still: our bed and breakfast with two double beds in a lovely old house. A wide verandah and small library. A cozy living room. The two of us marvel at this fresh new world and ourselves walking in it, hand in hand, *manus in manu*, as you, the Latin scholar, might say. I feel I'm right there, right now, and you're with me, so present, so alive. *Oh, Gordon! Gordon!* And I hasten back to my memories.

We leave this pretty town that's also the centre of the famous Marlborough wine region and are back to the wild black sands of western beaches on a hunt for someplace to stay the night.

Cape Foulwind, yes! This jutting shore fouled the progress even of Captain James Cook on his journey down its coast. In the early evening, we wander parts of its ragged coastline, and I think how the landmass that's New Zealand creates an obstruction to all west winds, and annoyed at being so thwarted, rage the more savagely.

Here, we find shelter in the spare bedroom of a family whose home stands perilously close to a line of pine trees brought to their knees by a ceaseless, indomitable west wind … *I never hear the west wind but tears are in my eyes.* And tears are in my eyes remembering this. In terms of beds, we enjoy an ordinary queen for our only night here. Our hosts, though, aren't particularly interested in us or our journey, and fleetingly I wonder if they're as bruised as their landscape by the furious elements.

This coast all but defies description; our experience of it is an intense one. I watch you lean into a wind blowing in from the Tasman Sea, observe the joy in your expression, the shine in your eyes — *free as I was to stand and stare* …

We find it hard to leave its jagged beauty, the compelling vistas of earth, sky, and sea, to move farther south. When I gaze at you, I wonder if you recall another, younger you, and how you travelled long and freely in your twenties, much the same way we're doing now, largely without plans and bookings, moving as you, and now we, feel the urge.

More stunning scenes come upon us one after another. We reach a coastal area called Punakaiki, known for its blowholes, and to the Pancake Rocks. You tell me these are formed from a mixture of compressed water and air that escape through caverns below and are forced upward. The resulting wall of spray is spectacular. Naturally, you want to know about the area's geological oddities, about rock formed thirty million years ago from minute fragments of dead marine creatures, as well as plants landing on the seabed. I feel your joy, your fascination, with the idea of the immense water pressure required to solidify the fragments into hard and soft layers, and how over time seismic action lifted the limestone above the seabed. Added to this are wind, sea water, and acidic rain, resulting in the bizarre shapes we see. Coastal forests, too, capture your interest, as well as the rich birdlife. I know your delight, not by your expressing it in words, but by the lift of your shoulders, the little smile that plays about your lips.

But it's time to move on, and we continue our trek south, arriving at quirky, funky little Greymouth. I've long had an attachment to semi-abandoned, half-forgotten places like this, and so I feel for this town that mourns its once-prosperous mining and jade-hunting past. We have the option of boarding a train to take us across the Southern Alps to Christchurch on the opposite coast, or to continue down the western shoreline. A difficult choice. We stick to our original plan and keep driving south.

The famous Franz Joseph Glacier — a World Heritage Site.

"Want to climb the glacier?" I ask you, teasing. "It'll have to be an ice walk — or we could go up in a helicopter." But the glacier has receded since it was explored in 1865, and all we can see from the village is a distant mountain with a sliding stretch of ice atop. All around us are rainforests, lakes, waterfalls, so we decide to stay the night.

Surprise! Exorbitant prices are asked for any accommodation, and not willing to pay them, we settle for twin beds in a gloomy, deserted motel on the town's outskirts. When confronted with the ridiculous cost of restaurants, we look at each other. By silent consensus, we search for a general store and buy packaged snack food and cans of pop. Returning to our run-down room, we sit swinging our legs on the rock-hard beds and have our dinner — a picnic of sorts. Next day dawns wet and cool, so we pass on.

Briefly, we stop at historic Hokitika. At its very name, I shiver as childhood images, perhaps myths, leap to mind. A place wild, unruly, lawless even, its reputation built in the 1860s by roaring waters and impenetrable bush, by tales of cutthroat gold hunters from all over the world, and by many ships known to have foundered on the notorious Hokitika Bar — really, a sandbar that shifts with every tide.

I tell you stories about the 1860s diggers of gold, those crumpled yellow-grey men coughing into the dust while clawing their way into this primeval, rotting jungle and sucked into tidal marshes. I search my memory for old news stories and gossip, for tales of the furious storms that raced up this coast, and feel myself shiver as a shadow seems to pass over the sun. We stand on a dirt path at the edge of the bush, listening to the thundering of distant water. I think for a moment that we'll drive into the town so I can better imagine the glitter and promise of this place, see the remnants of yesteryear: the huddled roofs of early dwellings, its port stuck in the crooked mouth of a river once rich in gold. As well, to look out over the infamous bar hiding three dozen and more wrecks.

"It's got a quaint little town a few miles east of here," I tell you, "but I'm not sure what's still there. It became prosperous for a while during and after the 1860s gold rush and should still have lovely old buildings and galleries. Oh, and it's also known for its greenstone jewellery."

An alertness comes over you at the mention of stones, rocks, gems. You look at me and ask, "So how about we go there and get you some stones?"

"Get *you* some, you mean. I don't need any. I've got you! Hey, here's an idea. Why don't we follow the Arahura River to where it enters the sea?" I pause for a moment, then add, "But we really don't have much time." Our deadline is to get back to the ferry terminal at Picton in twelve days.

One other mention of Hokitika: it's become famous through novelist

Eleanor Catton's multiple-award-winning novel *The Luminaries*, set here in the 1860s about a prospector attempting to make his fortune during the gold rush.

We decide to drive on, but I feel some disappointment that we haven't taken the time to go inland to see the town itself. But the little I've seen has fractured my childhood beliefs in the devils and dangerous spirits lurking here.

27

A Southern Journey

It's back into our rental car and on down the coastal highway. We take a detour into central Otago, the canyon-like rocky interior of South Island that was once rich in minerals, and a geographical antithesis of the coastal areas.

Queenstown, Arrowtown, both formerly rich gold-mining towns but now playgrounds of the rich and famous worldwide, home to some of the world's most famous people. Between them we find an Airbnb on a llama farm run by a lawyer and his wife. Well, this is interesting: the lawyer went as a young man to practise his profession on Norfolk Island. I've never been to this tiny place in the South Pacific but know it as a place defined by pine trees, jagged cliffs, and a ruined British penal colony. It's where author Colleen McCullough once lived when writing some of her novels.

We're vastly entertained by the lawyer and his wife, by their companionship with their animals. You're fascinated by creatures who refuse to foul their own place, using just one corner of their field as a toilet. A grey-speckled llama walks up to you and stretches its face right against yours as though to kiss you — who wouldn't want to do that? You also enjoy viewing the southern skies pasted over with a million stars.

What is to be our bed this time? Ordinary single ones, it seems.

To Queenstown, famous for being famous to the rich and famous, and ordinary mortals, as well, for good reason. Its physical beauty is said to be all but unparalleled anywhere in the world, but it has become almost exclusively touristy and caters to extreme sports seekers.

"Hey," I say, "let's go whitewater rafting. Or take a wild, high-speed ride on the Shotover River. Maybe go fishing or boating on the lake." I take your arm, and laughing up at you, say, "I know, you could go bungee jumping!"

Queenstown is where bungee jumping originated.

But we're too old for all this stuff and not interested. Fishing, whitewater rafting — we've done these things before.

We move on to quaint, neighbouring Arrowtown, once also a centre of the 1860s gold rush. Hand in hand, we wander its two streets and along the edge of the lake while the range of mountains known as The Remarkables looks benignly down on us.

Not being particularly interested in extreme sports or touristy knickknacks that are also expensive, we take a leisurely drive along the lonely shores of Lake Wanaka. When reaching its headwaters at Glen Orchy, we find an abandoned train station set up as a coffee bar and restaurant. Dinner that night includes roast beef sandwiches and local beer. Tiny, remote, in this idyllic spot, we dine on our sandwiches while inhaling the perfumes of flowering bushes. The hush surrounding us is interrupted only by birdsong. These glorious vistas are to me more captivating than either Queenstown or Arrowtown. Both of us nominate this drive, and this place, as one of the most beautiful in the world.

One afternoon, we arrive at Manapouri — think of rain at least fifty percent of the time, of rainforests, rugged coastlines, and high winds. Regardless, immediately, we set out to join a cruise along the famous fjord that is Doubtful Sound, which in fame and grandeur is second only to Milford Sound and so named because Captain Cook, seeking to enter, felt it too narrow and was thus thwarted.

You, Gordon, are intrigued to learn that the sound contains two distinct layers of water. In your inimitable way, you explain to me how fresh water on the top comes from run-off from the surrounding mountains, and below, a layer of salt water from the sea.

"The two don't mix," you say, "and that makes it difficult for light to penetrate. As a result, many deep-sea species like bottlenose dolphins and fur seals and penguins can be found here." To our great delight, we spot fur seals cavorting about the boat, penguins strutting the shoreline.

We continue our odyssey, as I think of it, right down to the southernmost coast, and cruise along it.

28

Where Are You?

Sometimes, as of right now, Gordon, I have profound heartache while writing this. I remember ... remember ... I'm seeing with your eyes and mine. I feel your hand in my hand. My brain registers along with yours the breadth and depth of my gorgeous, spectacular homeland. I see the two of us wandering its little towns, dreaming the same dream in all the lovely, bizarre, and strange beds we sleep in. I feel your heart beating, see your eyes brimming with intense interest and curiosity. Your love of being here with me washes over me again, and very emotional now, I hear myself call out to you, "Oh, Gordon! Gordon! Where are you?"

Relief comes only when in my mind I continue travelling ...

29

Another World Down Under

"Did you keep a diary?" asks a friend who's read the various drafts of my memoir. "Because if not, how do you remember all those details you've written?"

I don't have an answer. It must be because every moment we're there, every place we visit, I file away in some kind of mental and emotional archive, a psychic photograph album.

I see us now, you at the wheel driving us toward Invercargill. In obligation to a long-time friend in Toronto who grew up here, we roam this city with its deep Scottish roots — Irish, too — a city brimming with Victorian architecture. I try to imagine living in this, New Zealand's southernmost city so far removed from any significant place of habitation. I can so imagine because my own origins in North Island are also remote.

You decide to drive the day we leave Invercargill. The roads are excellent and largely devoid of other vehicles. You head us east toward Dunedin. On a lonely stretch of tarmac, I spy a large signpost leaning crookedly and say, "Hey, let's stop here."

We get out. *Wow!* We feel we're standing at the very edge of the world, nothing between us on this largely forgotten shoreline, and Antarctica — well, except for five little island groups that dot the Pacific where it meets the Tasman Basin: The Snares, Bounty, Antipodes, Auckland, and Campbell Islands.

A signpost shows us distances in miles to other parts of the world: Paris — 11,523 miles; Istanbul, almost 17,000; Toronto, 14,453.

We look at each other. A wind comes off the sea and slants the grasses, bends the stunted pine trees awkwardly toward the ocean. It blows your hair straight up on your head, and I ruffle it back in place with my hands, then kiss you. You've got that happy little smile on your face I love so much. Suddenly, you bend to pick me up and lift me high in the air. I stick out my tongue to catch the thickening salt off the sea, fling out my arms as though to catch the wind. We stand together there, our intimacy deepening as if to defy the isolation we feel.

"It really is lonely here," I say, "like we might not even exist, or if we did, who's to know when we stop — existing, that is."

We continue our trek eastward to Dunedin, you behind the wheel, your eyes alert as a lonely road stretches before us.

Dunedin is a city filled with memories for me, since I lived here for a year with my first husband, Graeme, while he attended the only medical school existing in New Zealand at that time. That particular year, 1966, he was a medical resident in the Departments of Internal Medicine and Rheumatology, while I worked in the Cadbury chocolate factory, as well as part-time as a psychiatric nurse before beginning a degree program at the University of Otago. My memories of that year are vivid. Small, quaint, and pretty, the city nestles among hills close to the ocean. It's known as New Zealand's Scottish city, the name Dunedin derived from the Gaelic for Edinburgh. I've always loved how its old stone buildings rise against sunlit hills.

To the east lies a peninsula that's home to both penguin and albatross colonies. Occasionally, rare sea lions are glimpsed. Naturally, we tour these sites.

We hang around the far reaches of the peninsula — so lonely here, too — waiting for an albatross to reveal itself. You, Gordon, are particularly interested in these rare birds that spend most of their lives at sea, and here you are at the only mainland breeding colony of royal albatrosses existing in the world.

Patiently, we wait for a parent albatross to leave the nest so we can admire its nine-foot wingspan. Eventually, we're rewarded.

You stand beside me, silent and smiling, profoundly moved by this.

"Spectacular!" I say for both of us.

Afterward, we drive into the hills above Dunedin where drifts a light mist. The roads are narrow and twisting. The higher we climb the more thickly the mist falls, all but obscuring the landscape. Scraggly willow and kowhai trees jump out as ghostly apparitions, and the landscape's sudden peaks and hollows makes it eerie, also a little frightening. Suddenly, we reach a peak, and the ground disappears abruptly on the other side, dropping steeply among grassy slopes dotted with grazing sheep.

But it's the trees, too, that I remember. Altogether it has an amazing diversity of plants, animals, and habitats, most of which aren't found anywhere else in the world.

Ah, New Zealand! I wanted to leave it, didn't want to live here again, but I love to visit it and am deeply moved by all I'm seeing, showing it off almost as though I owned it. I remember how my mother loved her country, her place on God's earth, and if you lived here, why would you bother visiting somewhere else? When filing a census form required by the government, she refused to identify herself as "European" and listed "Other" in its place, meaning "Kiwi."

We leave Dunedin to begin the long drive up the east coast, stopping at small coastal towns on the way, including Oamaru, known for its little blue penguins, pottery, and Victorian architecture. Then Timaru and on to Christchurch where we plan to stay two nights. This we've actually organized in advance, unusual for the two of us who like to wander unhindered by dates, times, and bookings.

30

Us at Home

I'm in the rocking chair that once belonged to your mother, thinking about you, not the two of us travelling right now but us at home. But when am I not? I think about all the funny, intimate things we did together and the events and habits that made up our life.

Your head cradled in my arms, I, getting breakfast in bed.

"I just love you so much," I say.

"Likewise," you reply, which eventually becomes "I love you, too."

"What show would you like to see tonight? A movie?"

"Let's go out for dinner."

Later, you driving to the airport at 2:00 a.m. to pick up my sister's granddaughter, allowing my insomniac self to remain in bed.

You, up early on Sunday mornings to drive your niece, Anik, to hockey games.

And, oh, the memory of a night at a Beethoven symphony concert, and afterward, you ask, "What about going for sushi?"

"Okay!"

Hand in hand, we walk along King Street toward Yonge, south to Front Street, and into a crowded sushi restaurant. Afterward, you ask, "How about a taxi home?"

Not a big deal, but to many in our generation it isn't the custom to just jump into a cab. I think that surely I'm in heaven.

Sometimes now I get up and put on your navy blue cardigan with the zipper. I also recall the times I trimmed your eyebrows, rubbed lotion on your feet, inserted those wretched little things in your eyes for your dry-eye condition. I have visions of you coming out of the shower, searching your sock drawer, getting a T-shirt.

Early in our relationship, we're at a movie and I want to hold your hand. But you lean back in your chair, so totally engrossed that you wouldn't notice if the world ended. Learning, reading, absorbing information is almost all of life for you.

How, then, did you see me? How did you fall in love with me? I've quoted George Eliot who says in *Middlemarch*: "We are not afraid of telling over and over again how a man comes to fall in love with a woman and be wedded to her, or else be fatally parted from her."

Our story is that we found perfect love late in life. We wedded, and after a brief ten, eleven years, were fatally parted.

You said I'm the most enthusiastic person you've ever known. The following lighthearted little poem written for me by my daughter and granddaughters for a special birthday gives a glimpse of me, this woman you so loved:

> There once was a girl from Te Pahu
> Who dreamed of great things she could do:
> So she hopped on a plane
> And was never the same,
> As off to Toronto she flew.
> Carolyn is the great multi-tasker
> Who loves to do everything faster.
> For her friends she will cook
> While writing a book
> At which she became quite a master.
>
> Then one day Carolyn got bored,
> But luckily she then met Gord.
> They got along while singing a song,
> And Carolyn felt she had scored.
>
> Carolyn's friends and family really love her.
> She's lively, kind, and a great mother.

She will help out in a pinch,
To her everything's a cinch ...

I, this woman, like *Mrs Dalloway* in Virginia Woolf's novel, love life. In the book, Peter Walsh asks Mrs Dalloway why she gives so many parties. She says it's because she loves life; it's her gift. You, too, could ask me, "What does this mean to you, these evenings of entertainment you give?" My answer is that it's a sense of the existence of other people and putting them together. As with Mrs Dalloway, it's my offering.

Then death comes. And how soon, how soon it's all over, and I never do get an answer about how you came to see me, to notice me.

31

Christchurch

It's a cool, rainy day, and I'm lying across my bed attempting to listen to CBC Radio when suddenly, at the mention of New Zealand, an image of the two of us there catches me unawares: we're in a restaurant in the heart of Christchurch, a city that had large parts of it demolished during a massive earthquake ten years earlier. I revisit the day, the evening, when we're googling the few restaurants where we might dine, choosing one and setting out to walk the mile distant. The two of us move in the dusk among ghosts that lurk in broken buildings, I, busy imagining mannequins in abandoned stores laughing behind our backs, seeing their shadows flit before us in the deepening dusk. You say nothing, only take in everything about you. The restaurant is a revelation. Large, imposing even, its wide, arched entrance leads to an enormous room separated into halves. The waiter appraises us, then gestures to an area to the left. The majority of diners are to the right.

Why? I wonder. Then I see: we're dressed casually as are the few diners to the left. Those on the right have attired themselves as though for a ball, the men wearing suits and ties, the women in frosted hairstyles, and as I cast my eyes further, catch sight of their stiletto-heeled shoes. Really! How can they possibly walk in the city's rubble in those?

It's that image of the two of us smiling at each other as though complicit in something no one else understands that impinges, and a powerful wish to return there, to that road trip, overshadows anything on CBC Radio. I close my eyes and allow my mind to return to that blighted city, to finish the final episode in our South Island odyssey.

Christchurch, named after Christ's College, Cambridge, also called Garden City, is known for its botanic gardens and many parks, for its riverbanks and flowering walkways. Not least for the River Avon that runs through it. In 2011, the city was devastated by an earthquake with a magnitude of 6.3, killing one hundred and eighty-five people, injuring several thousand and severely damaging many of its most beautiful old stone and brick buildings to make an area more than four times the size of London's Hyde Park instantly uninhabitable.

Our drive into its centre in search of accommodation is like entering a moonscape. The heart of the city was reduced to rubble, with only a building here and there bravely or sullenly rising above the devastation all around it. My hand flies to my mouth in shock, and both of us remain in awed silence.

Our accommodation is in the only standing building in the city's old heart that's judged to be safe and is reinforced. At its feet runs a small train on wheels to a shopping centre built of old shipping containers, then back again in a loop. It stands in proximity to the city's main cathedral that crouches battered and broken in the middle of the main square. A newly consecrated cardboard cathedral stands beside it. And on an area of vacant land alongside are one hundred and eighty-five chairs arranged in rows to represent the number of people killed.

We walk among the broken buildings, peer in abandoned shop windows. Suddenly, I jump back. "Hey, there are dead people standing around in there!"

You don't even turn around. When you do, it's with an expression of amusement.

"Really! Come and look for yourself."

You walk over, and together we peer through the smudged glass.

Five lifelike mannequins stand in various poses, staring back at us. One lies on the floor, its arms flung out. Another is decked in summer clothes, while others are naked.

We laugh and keep on walking. But in my mind, I'm already constructing a story for the mannequins.

Sorrow for this place weighs on us: for the loss of life, for the beautiful Georgian brick buildings that stand bowed, condemned. In a shopping area beyond the city centre, we ask a clerk how she feels living in what in effect is a ghost city.

"We've heard that many people have moved permanently elsewhere within New Zealand," I say.

"Oh, but we have faith in our city," the young woman tells us. "We'll never leave it, never desert it."

What courage and faith in the future!

The next day, we wander about the botanical gardens and linger in Hagley Park. How we love this place for its old trees, the river flowing through it, its quiet grace, but sorrow lingers at the sight of the destroyed buildings dotted about. Time is running out. We have to leave this desolate city to travel on and up the coast toward Picton to meet my old neighbours, to travel with them across Cook Strait and back up North Island.

And so north along the coast we drive. I will only mention Kaikoura, a small town cradled on the coast between awe-inspiring mountains on one side and the ocean on the other. Sadly, there's no time for whale-watching.

That afternoon we can't make the trip on the ferry across Cook Strait. The storm-tossed waters throw up waves more than eighteen feet high. Gale-force winds are forecast. We have to stay overnight with the hope of calmer waters the next day. This crossing, from Wellington to Picton, gives spectacular panoramic views of Wellington Harbour at the southern end of North Island, and the stunning natural waterways of the Marlborough Sounds of South Island. In between lies Cook Strait. And here the Tasman Sea meets the Pacific in tumultuous greeting. Next morning, we enjoy one of the world's most scenic and exhilarating ferry journeys, then begin the hours-long drive up North Island.

32

Portugal

It's late March when we return to Toronto. We empty our suitcases, launder our summer clothes, then pack them back in our suitcases.

"Are we really doing this?" We look at each other, laugh, and keep on packing. Two weeks later, wanderlust still in our blood, we leave for Portugal with three friends while still suffering the effects of jet lag.

Why do we engage in all this travel? What drives us to explore so far and for so long? The pure exhilaration of adventure, of course. The joy of discovering other places and their histories. Not least, learning how other people live, hearing different languages. Self-knowledge, too, perhaps. We're perfectly in tune with each other to an uncanny degree, perfectly matched in everything we think and do and what we want. It might be called synchronicity, synergy. Complicity. Whatever it is, it works!

The beaches of northern Portugal are windswept and cold. We freeze. We have only the summer clothes we wore in midsummer New Zealand. And so we go shopping for cardigans and jackets. What kind of beds this time? Comfortable single ones in a spacious apartment where we step out our front door directly onto the street. I love that!

We wander ancient Nazaré where little seems to have changed over the centuries, largely because the only times this little fishing town sees tourists are when international surfing competitions take place.

Our days are unscheduled, unplanned, exactly how we like to travel, and that reminds me of your early wanderlust days in Southeast Asia, Gordon. Then, as now, time was your own. What you did was what you felt like at each moment; you obeyed your own inner rhythms.

In a rental car, we travel to the Sanctuary of Our Lady of Nazaré. This fascinates: an imposing Marian shrine founded in the fourteenth century memorializing a miracle involving the Virgin Mary. We also check out Memory Hermitage, known also as the Chapel of Our Lady of Nazaré. What a dramatic location, perched right on the edge of a promontory high above the city. And what a remarkable building with its pyramidal roof and four-sided chapel.

Two weeks later, we're on our way to the Azores, then home.

33

Toronto Afterward

It's the coming home — from anywhere — when your absence hits me hardest, Gordon. Every corner of our house has you in it, and when I'm not distracted, I feel fragile, abandoned. Lonely, too. I remember the day I go to buy Rudolph's bread at Loblaws in the former Maple Leaf Gardens — you always walked over there to get it — but I can't find it and ask a clerk where it is.

"What kind?" the clerk asks.

"What kind? I don't know!"

He points to a rack and shrugs.

When I still can't find it, tears spring to my eyes and I stumble home, crying all the way. But then I'm always crying. Sometimes when I doze, I half dream you're on your way back from a walk or some appointment, only to realize you'll never be home again. I go outside to wander the streets. I see a man who resembles you coming toward me: tall, grey hair, moustache, and think it's you. "Oh, oh!" I hold my breath. But the feeling of euphoria is gone in a split second, immediately replaced by sorrow. I think that I can't do this; how can I do this? I loved, loved you! We were perfect together, always together. I can't think of memories right now; the pain, the sorrow, are far too deep.

Eventually, perhaps later that day or the next, I decide to do some writing. After an hour at my desk editing a story I've provisionally entitled "A Man Called George" — an excellent distraction — I'm about to call up the stairs, "Are you hungry and ready for lunch?" Silence from up there. I go downstairs, but you're not in your chair in front of the TV watching Wimbledon, taking in the news or a science program. You're not anywhere, and again I wonder how I can do this.

It's another night, and I'm on my way to have dinner with friends, but tears are in my eyes all the time. I cry out to the empty walls, the vacant doorways, the empty doors, the chair upstairs where you died. *Where are you?* "No! No, no, no!" I hear my voice echoing down the two flights of stairs. "How could you have left me? How *could* you?"

34

Istanbul

What to do? Travel in memory once more, find some escape from this heartache. I've been rereading some of Persian poet Rumi's poems — "After despair comes hope, and sunlight over all the hills" — and decide it will be to Turkey, since that's where Rumi spent most of his life. The Turks are a people I love, and Turkey is a place that resonates deeply because of the research I did for my novel *Helena*.

What joy to plan this visit — yes, we actually organize parts of it, which isn't generally our habit. As well as seeing the homes and landscapes of my characters in *Helena*, you ask me, "Where else in Turkey would you like to go?"

"Istanbul," I say at once, getting immediate agreement.

Istanbul, historic Constantinople. Its name conjures great and terrible events, its buildings, landscape, testimony to an ancient story punctuated by terrible wars that altered history. One could suppose it was deliberately designed to be the capital of the world: once Greek, then Roman, then Byzantine, then Ottoman, its power remaining in Turkey and echoing the world over. In a short walk, one can find a Roman inscription, a Byzantine wall, an Ottoman fountain; in a few steps, one passes between different civilizations, feels the city's pulse, its weight, its style and grandeur. Spectacular views are everywhere.

Like many tourists, we stay in Sultanahmet. From there, we tour the great Turkish bazaar and Topkapi Palace. How we pity those on tourist buses who crowd themselves into each historic place, hurry from one site to another: five minutes here, a few more moments there, then back on the bus perhaps fifteen minutes later.

We're in the magnificent Hagia Sophia with its four minarets, learning its history. Someone says that for many centuries after the Ottoman conquest of the city, after the basilica's first conversion from Christian church to mosque, old Greek women wailed outside its walls. It then became a museum, reverting to a mosque, a museum again, and now a mosque once more. It's a meeting point of the world's religions, its walls a blend of Islamic art and symbols of Christianity that serve as a centre of religious, political, and artistic life for the Eastern Orthodox world. Its importance was, and is, infinite, its magnificent architecture all but indescribable. Sometimes a picture might really be worth a thousand words.

Outside, on an old stone wall, we sit swinging our legs in the sunshine. A young man approaches us, perches himself beside us, and immediately begins chatting in perfect English.

"My name is Mehmed," he says. "I'm a Kurd."

My eyes open wide. A Kurd: images leap in the air of rangy horsemen, tough, warlike millions of them cursed with having no homeland of their own and destined not to have one in any foreseeable future. Mehmed: a young man swaying his legs alongside us, asking about ourselves. Seduced into conversation, we remain there until the sun slides lower in the sky, until Mehmed jumps from the wall and offers to take us on tour of the Blue Mosque, officially known as Sultan Ahmed Mosque.

Oh! Into my mind spring bits of my knowledge of the sultan after whom the mosque is named — Ahmed I, a young man following upon the legacy of great leaders such as Suleiman the Magnificent or Mehmed the Conqueror. What weight of history on this young man's thin shoulders! We trail this modern-day Mehmed to the imposing, elegant Blue Mosque with its ascending domes and six slender, soaring minarets.

"A classical Ottoman structure," Mehmed says, as I'm sure he's quoted countless times before. At its entrance, once our shoes are removed and before we enter, he says, "You Christians have what you call a Trinity — God, Jesus, and ... a ghost. A ghost!" He repeats this and laughs.

"Well, a spirit," I say, not joining in his laughter.

Curious rather than offended, afterward, we allow ourselves to be persuaded to visit his family's carpet shop. It's warm but not hot. I wear long skirts, sometimes jeans and a peasant blouse. You, Gordon, have finally ditched your many-pocketed shorts that come to your knees and now look tall and lean in simple, shorter shorts, with T-shirts or short-sleeved shirts, most of them blue.

We follow Mehmed along dusty streets, having not yet learned that this carpet-selling business is widespread and practised by carpet sellers all over Turkey. Many who have visited any town in this country will know the sequence of events that follows: the sudden proliferation of men who seem to appear out of nowhere, the rush to find us chairs, a cup of tea or cool drink offered with warm hospitality. Then the beginning of prolonged persuasive and intense efforts to have us purchase a carpet. Even if we were so inclined, how can we possibly choose among many thousands presented, their corners flipped up? To refuse is to walk away feeling guilty, obligated at the effort and time they've devoted to this end.

Through long corridors and intricate pathways, we walk the Turkish Bazaar, an indescribable assault on all the senses — so much to see, so much to choose, if we can! In the end, we purchase very little.

In Sultanahmet, we see a poster advertising a rooftop garden. DOUBLE RAKI, TWO FOR THE PRICE OF ONE proclaims the ad. And so up to the rooftop restaurant we climb to find a table revealing views over the city on one side and that great waterway, the Bosporus, on the other. We each order a double raki, and from the menu, some smoky kebabs, a dish of vegetables, and pilaf.

It's now late afternoon. The Bosporus signals the end of the West and the beginning of the East. Mesmerized, we gaze over its choppy waters, busy with ferries, water taxis, freighters, and other large vessels from around the world. On the other side under a fitful sun, Istanbul spreads out to seeming infinity. Our senses sharpen. We're on the edge of a great history — well, an ancient one. We're gazing at it, feeling joy in sharing it. We order another two-for-one raki.

Sharp at five o'clock, the muezzin at the Blue Mosque signals the *adhan*, or in Turkish, the *ezan*, the call to prayer. *Adhan* or *ezan* means "to listen, to hear, to be informed about." Immediately following the Blue Mosque's rhythmic chanting comes a cascade from smaller mosques all over the city, sounding out their calls to prayer one after another after another. I'm enchanted, you equally so. "Hey, let's have another raki each," I suggest.

From the young waiter, we order yet another round. He looks at us, and through his eyes, I see an elderly couple, innocent, unsophisticated, obviously in love, and this makes me smile at you, Gordon. Your returning one has a familiar hint of mischief in it.

"He sees this old couple up on the roof getting drunk and wonders if he should actually give them another round," I say. "Give me a kiss, old man." And I lean across the table.

"There's one place I really want to see," you say.

"What?"

"Istanbul's Cistern."

"Oh, yes, the famous subterranean cistern called the Basilica. I've vaguely heard about it."

We locate it under a large public square on the First Hill of Constantinople. Here, between the third and fourth centuries CE, a great basilica stood and acted as the commercial, legal, and artistic centre of the city. Ancient texts indicate that it once contained gardens surrounded by a colonnade facing the Hagia Sophia.

You love all this! We spend a long time in the Cistern reading every word: texts claiming that seven thousand slaves were involved in the construction of it. About the enlarged Cistern providing a water filtration system for the Great Palace of Constantinople. About other buildings, too, on the First Hill that continued to provide water right into modern times.

We almost miss the massive sculpture of Medusa's head that lies upside down underwater at the far western corner of the Cistern. Huge, riveting, we can see her from many angles, her mouth twisted in that famous pout, eyes crossed. Again, a picture, a photo, is sometimes worth a thousand words. Knowing the story of Medusa, I'm stuck to the spot, gazing at her with awe. Eventually, we have to move on, but for my sake, you take many photos of her.

"Okay, where to next?" you ask.

"Ankara," I say.

Of course, Turkey's capital, two hundred and eighty-five miles southeast of Istanbul and an eight-hour overnight train ride.

"But we won't see the landscape," I protest.

"Plenty more to see," you say, and promptly fall asleep on the top bunk bed.

Visions of Ankara's ancient, huge, crumbling stone gate to its famous citadel come to me, but we don't know how to get to it and have no time, anyway, since we're to meet Üstün Bilgen-Reinart and her husband, Jean, in the old city for dinner.

Ankara, both a new and a very ancient city. It's in a spartan bed we sleep that night in the old city. After a day and a half, we leave Ankara and randomly get on public buses to criss-cross the vast spaces that make up the Turkish landscape: mountain ranges closer to the east, an endless windswept steppe, then to the strange and bizarre contours of Cappadocia in central Turkey.

Those journeys on Turkey's buses are adventures in themselves. The efficiency and cleanliness are awesome. Every two hours, we stop at a mini-paradise: gardens of climbing roses, little shops, and toilets of both the European and Asian type. Our bus is washed down inside and out. Only then do we resume our journey.

Difficulty comes when the driver stops his bus alongside a smaller one and gestures to a few of us who are non-Turks. We don't understand, and you, Gordon, say we should remain on the bus. The driver checks his passengers once more before driving on, sees us, gestures wildly, and speaks incomprehensibly. The smaller bus is moving off. Our driver races out of his bus and yells at the disappearing driver until he stops. His gestures to us are now unmistakable — "You're to get off this bus and onto that one."

So, my beloved, I can see you're not right all the time.

35

Cappadocia, Turkey

And so we travel to the part of Anatolia called Cappadocia.

"Fully booked, I'm sorry," says the clerk at a check-in centre. "You haven't reserved anything?" Incredulity spreads over his face.

We look at each other, feeling foolish.

"Well, let me see." The boyish clerk in jeans and T-shirt walks over to another booth, consults a colleague, and again runs his eyes over his lists. He gives us a penetrating stare, then comes to a decision. "I'm giving you the sultan's palace, the king's honeymoon suite," he says, suddenly smiling. "You can have another honeymoon."

"We're still having one," I say, delighted.

Lost to me is what else he says as I gaze at you with a rush of love. Every moment, I feel chosen, celebrated, alive, always at the edge of something huge. All those fine lines around your eyes, your lips — are they an accumulation of laughter, of disappointment? How I love to look at you. "Our honeymoon? It'll never be over," I say with conviction.

A sultan's palace, indeed! A magnificent rock dwelling, it has several balconies giving us views of the strange moonscape surrounding us from all sides. Inside is a king-sized bed, but it looks tiny in the cavernous space. Scattered about are ottomans, rock tables, chairs, armoires ...

In the king bed, I say, "Hey, I can't find you! Where are you?" Laughing, I search under mounds of soft Egyptian cotton sheets. Next morning, we arrange with a private tour guide to travel over the rocky landscape that extends beyond Monk's Valley to Göreme. Everywhere we see Bronze Age homes of soft volcanic rock carved into the valley walls. Cave churches, too, and home as well to troglodytes who are known to have lived underground.

In the area farther north, we tour the vast underground city that once housed more than twenty thousand Hittites. These were very early Indo-Europeans who lived here to protect themselves from marauders. We climb down and down, two hundred and thirty-six feet beneath the earth's surface in this city with its eighteen descending levels. The troglodytes who also once lived here had fresh water, oil presses, stables, and great vaults, as well as places for the worship of their storm gods. Massive rolling stone doors were shut when enemies were spotted on the horizon.

We're silent, in awe that this huge underground city has existed for three thousand years. Greeks, too, have lived in caves dotted all over Cappadocia, right up until 1923.

Most readers will be familiar with this unusual World Heritage Site, which appears in leaflets, brochures, glossy magazines, travel agents' material, and travelogues the world over. Göreme and Monk's Valley are well known for their eerie landscapes, often called fairy chimneys — rock formations that pop up randomly over what looks like a moonscape.

Now on our own, we travel on buses around the countryside, both moved and saddened by the number of old Greek houses, orchards, and surrounding gardens that were abandoned when local Greeks, having lived here for centuries, were forced out of Turkey and into poor parts of Greece — to them an alien country and people. How ornamental their houses, how lovingly tended, and now, about a hundred years later, how overgrown, rusting, and rotting. For reasons not known to us, Turks haven't taken them over.

How privileged I feel for having wandered over this landscape with you, Gordon, and for however briefly, inserting myself into its long history. We're seeing everything together with one heart, one mind.

"Where would you like to go now?" you ask me.

Thinking of the trail of my fictional characters, I say, "Kayseri."

This distant city farther east is difficult to get to on buses and therefore time-consuming, so instead I choose the southern city of Konya, known also as Turkey's religious city. Then begins the scramble to find a ticket office and a bus depot.

The city, a pilgrimage destination for Sufis, is focused on the tomb of Rumi, the founder of the Mevlevi Order. Immediately, we set out for the Mevlâna Museum complex in the centre of Konya, which also includes Rumi's mausoleum. Then it's on to the nearby twelfth-century Alâeddin Mosque, surrounded by the green parkland of Alâeddin Hill. As we've done in other cities, we chat to each other as we stroll the streets. Suddenly, a young man comes alongside and addresses us in English.

"My name is Mehmed …"

A popular name, I think.

Then comes his astonishing comment to me. "I know where you're from."

"Where?"

"New Zealand."

What! How can this possibly be? He explains that he once had a girlfriend from New Zealand and recognized my accent. Sadly, for him, the girl refused to come to live with him in Turkey, even though he promised that if she did, they'd relocate to Istanbul and she wouldn't have to wear a hijab.

• • •

Konya is the place where you, Gordon, get the haircut and shave of your life, and how we both enjoy that! In a rented room in a poor part of the city, from our window, we watch the busy street below, spot heavily cloaked local people wait for buses to take them home after a day's work.

At the barbershop, the owner's face spreads into a huge grin when he catches sight of us. Pushing his current clients out of their chairs, he beckons us in, and bowing and smiling, ushers you to a chair. Then he hustles to find a plastic one for me and proceeds to make tea. Only after that does he get to work on his Anglo customer, no doubt a rare find in this poor working-class part of the city. You're given the whole works in traditional Turkish fashion: hot, wet towels, candle flames to nose and ears, a sharp razor cut. I laugh at the sight of you emerging as fresh and scrubbed as a newborn of any species.

Open markets display many hundreds of coloured scarves among other items, so I purchase one to the nodding approval of the salesman — all salesmen are male, even in women's clothing and underwear shops. I knew that, but even so it's unsettling.

36

Spectral Images

Unsettling? I'm feeling unsettled after awaking from a dream, actually, a nightmare. In it, I see a waif-like bride in a short bridal dress, and I follow her to her wedding feast. When I get there, the bridal table is empty, but I sit down, anyway. Then, out of the corner of my eye, I glimpse a man walking toward me, and my heart stops. It's you, Gordon! Seating yourself opposite, you smile at me with love-filled eyes.

"How beautiful you are," I say, returning your smile, only to find myself confronted with a stranger.

Where on earth has this come from? My eyes are wet. In the cobbly light of early morning, disturbed, I get up and walk to the window. The world outside appears whitewashed, and I register that it rained during the night — consonant with my mood, I think.

I've long wondered why I haven't dreamed about you more often, Gordon. But I've read that the dead who are ever-present in the minds of the bereaved often don't dream of their loved ones.

I think that if I return to my travels with you, maybe I can erase those upsetting images, so I wrap myself in your dressing gown, trudge upstairs to your old office, now mine, to take myself back to Konya, leave it, and journey toward the mountainous city of Afyon.

OUR PHOTO ALBUM

Gordon, Noranda.

Gordon, Noranda.

The Watts family home in Cobalt.

Gordon's parents, Marjorie and Murray Watts.

Gordon as a young man.

Gordon in South Korea.

Gordon's graduation photo from St. Michael's College.

Gordon's youthful travels throughout Asia.

Gordon travelling in Asia.

Gordon in Australia.

Gordon and his son, Matt.

Colleagues Scott Griffiths (left), Lee Barker, Gordon, John Parry (right) at Gull Lake, 1966, preparing for a rugby game.

Will you marry me?

A knot made in paradise.

Gordon and Carolyn in Raglan, New Zealand.

On a boat in the Toronto harbour.

OUR TRAVELS IN TURKEY

In Afyon, high in the mountains of central Turkey.

In Cappadocia.

TRAVELS IN NEW ZEALAND

Gordon and Carolyn in New Zealand.

Glen Orchy, South Island, New Zealand.

Milford Sound.

Gordon on a farm in New Zealand's Waikato.

Gordon in New Zealand's Northland.

37

In the Mountains of Central Turkey

Leaving Konya, we venture by bus even farther into Turkey's seldom-travelled regions, arriving in Afyon, high in the mountains of central Turkey. In Turkish, *afyon* means "opium," and perhaps that's the reason the city has been known formally since 2004 as Afyonkarahisar, the same name for the Citadel that looms above it.

"This is just an exotic place to visit," I say to you, explaining my choice. "My fictional family didn't come from here nor live here."

Exotic Afyon is. Considered a gateway between the Aegean Sea and the inner regions of Anatolia, it sits at the crossroads of three different areas of Turkey. The mountainous topography surrounding it means hot, dry summers, mild, rainy springs, and cold, snowy winters.

Where to stay? The night before we left Konya, you googled accommodations in this hilltop city and located a converted Muslim mansion. We should have read the guidebooks! They advise prospective travellers to avoid such places for good reason. Rain comes in under the one window in our room. The sheets are threadbare — no blanket — and the tiny room is cold. I go downstairs to the office to ask for a blanket, but alas, can't communicate. The woman on duty thinks I'm complaining that the sheets are dirty. Finally, we receive not a blanket but one extra sheet. A tiny cubicle contains the toilet, a hand basin, and a shower head attached to one wall. To take a shower means the entire cubicle becomes soaked. About to pick up the hair dryer off its hook on the wall, I realize I'm standing in about an inch of water.

"I almost electrocuted myself!" I yell.

But Turkish people are without exception wonderful. When we amble about Afyon's sloping streets, heads swivel and stare after us; apparently, people in this remote region have never heard another language, never seen a tourist. We tiptoe through the steep, muddy cobblestone streets after a rainfall, around a corner, and there at the top, spy a family gathered for a picnic. Perhaps it's a celebration of some kind, but we'll never know because we can't communicate. Only when they see our two Western faces peeping around the corner do they beckon us. As we pick our way up to join them, a young man rushes to find rickety plastic chairs for us, a plastic table. Then a woman brings a steaming bowl of stew to put before us, along with one spoon.

"Share a bed, share a spoon, we'll share everything, my beloved," I tell you.

We watch as a young man plays a guitar, another a viola while dancing over the rain-soaked cobblestones. At the same time, black-cloaked women run about with their many children, smiling broadly and gesturing, but we can't find a way to communicate other than to say, "Thank you, thank you," in English, then in Turkish.

• • •

"Afyon is three thousand years old," I tell you after some reading. "Did you know it's been home to Hittites, Lydians, Persians, Greeks, Romans, Byzantines, Seljuks, and Ottomans?"

"That's all?" you say with that little smile of yours, then turn to the Internet for more details of the city's history.

We learn Afyon is famed for a specific type of Turkish delight, for a kind of hard cream poured on desserts, and for its opium fields, now under strict supervision by the government. You, of course, are interested in the city's quarries, thermal baths, and Citadel. The last sits atop a hill rising sharply from the centre of Afyon.

"The Citadel was once used as a fortress by the Hittite king Mursilis II," you quote. "Afyonkarahisar, it's known as in Turkish — literally Black Opium Castle in English." So the Citadel dates back as far as 1350 BCE.

You climb the highest peak as nimbly as a mountain goat, swift-limbed and supple. I get only halfway up.

"What a view!" Your eyes shine when you reach me on your way down.

Before returning to the Ottoman "mansion," we sit on a bench in a public park. Across from us is a family of several generations enjoying a picnic in the sun. They come over and offer us food and drinks. Ah, Turkey and Turkish people: the finest, warmest, most hospitable of any we've encountered.

Before we leave Afyon, we walk its damp, cobblestone streets, see Turkish men sitting in the sunlight outside local stores in the mornings and throughout the afternoons. We chat with each other as we stroll. Again, heads swivel and many pairs of eyes stare at us. As before in Konya, I suppose they've never heard another language.

38

Izmir

"Where would you like to go now?" you ask me.

"Izmir," I say at once, my heart leaping. At long last! This, for me, is a near-mythical city where for many years I've lived in my imagination, online, in books, and in general research. So by bus we travel across Turkey all the many hours to Izmir.

Smyrna, now Izmir, is an ancient mercantile city on the Mediterranean coast with more than three thousand years of history, a place of infidels to which Turkey's prime minister never travels because it's said he can't bear the sight of bare-headed women, of people drinking and enjoying themselves in sidewalk cafés.

It's urgent that I get to the waterfront in this jewel of a city. In part, my heart belongs here, my mind weighted with its history, with the tragedy that befell many thousands of its citizens as in my fictional family in *Helena*. I wrote the entire novel without seeing Izmir's waterfront, its docks, any of it. In my imagination, I've lived here. My great challenges have been the questions: How did two peasants and their father from impoverished central Turkey make a living in this place? How did they live in this city, on this waterfront, where their fate was determined?

I stand where once a ghastly history played out. Blue-green swells of the Aegean swirl around a wooden pier that extends into the sea, then curl softly onto shore. On those docks, on that beach, people now cast fishing lines. I've been here in my mind over the many years writing my story. Today, people walk, chat, fish. As I stare at this contemporary scene, suddenly, I'm not registering it anymore. Instead, I glimpse a time almost a hundred years before when the waters weren't calm, the fishermen weren't relaxed, and visitors didn't stroll a peaceful waterfront. Right here, many thousands of Turkish-Greeks were shot, slaughtered, and drowned.

Fishing! I want to scream, "Stop! Don't you know what's down there?" To my astonishment, the waters turn crimson, screams fill my ears, the harbourfront is in flames. I catch sight of the blood-red Turkish flag with its star and crescent tilting against heavy columns of smoke. Non-Turks rush to the waterfront to escape the fires raging behind them. Idling out in the bay are ships from many nations, including the British dreadnoughts *King George V*, *Iron Duke*, and *Ajax*; the French *Ernest Renan*; and the American destroyers *Litchfield* and *Edsall*.

People continue to jump into the sea to escape the brutality on the shore, to flee from the guns firing at them. Some try to clamber up the sides of the Western ships in the harbour but are booted back into the water, most of them drowning. The sea runs red with their blood. I'm right back in my novel *Helena*, and those fishermen with their lines in the water could be hauling up dead bodies. Now I feel sick.

You, my darling, walk with me, shelter me from my emotions as I imagine the horror that occurred here. You're there beside me, telling me, "It's okay, okay," as I slowly return to the present, to a waterfront unchanged in structure from those years but now tranquil with tourists and local families.

Taking me to the markets, to upscale shops, to the Museum of History & Art in the Kültürpark, you photograph everything for me.

There's another place I must see — the suburb in the hills once called Bournabat, now Bournova, where my fictional family moved once they were financially secure. Wherever I want to go, you want to go, too. A warm memory returns of our trek to those hilly suburbs. Not knowing how to pay to use the train, we stand looking at each other, perplexed, when two young local Turks come up and with gestures ask us where we're going. I utter the name Bournova. The next moment, they've paid for us and are handing us our tickets.

Our beds those nights in Izmir are low and hard, but we're close to the clock tower on the city's promenade that so rivets me in a city that entrances me.

39

Flying Home

We fly on a Turkish airline called Pegasus back to Istanbul and so to home. When I see you settled in your seat, phone in one hand, seemingly comfortable, I ask, "What are you looking so happy about?" (I dislike flying.)

"Just that I don't have any more responsibilities," you reply.

Oh! It's then that I realize the effort, the stress, incurred in what you've done for us: *What would you like to do? Where do you want to go now?* And you would begin an Internet search to find accommodation for the next day, hunt for a ticket office, find out how to get to it, and then locate a bus to take us to wherever I've indicated — all this while trying to make yourself understood. *Thank you, Gordon!*

40

Love That Lasts a Million Years

My joy in remembering and writing all this is tinged with an overlay of a now-familiar sense of immeasurable loss. At each morning awakening, I feel flat. In a blue mood after returning from revisiting this period of lives, I flop on my/our bed and weep until I sleep. I dream I'm with you on holiday somewhere at a beach. I'm lying in a rented cottage, crying uncontrollably. I lift my head and ask a faded figure that looks like you, "Are you a ghost? Don't you miss Gordon, too?"

"But you *are* Gordon!" I exclaim. And then you're not. You hover faintly, then retreat. Half back in that dream, I think I should get up and do something, not waste that holiday; I should see a famed beach I've heard about. While walking toward it, my phone rings, and suddenly I'm awake and weeping because the dream has gone. You're gone.

I'm crying too much. But how much is too much? And I remember a passage, but from where I can't remember. It goes like this:

> There is sadness in tears
> They are not the mark of
> Weakness, but of power.
> They speak more eloquently
> Than a hundred tongues.
> They are messengers of
> Overwhelming grief, of deep
> Contrition and of unspeakable love.

Our bedroom, our bed, is my sanctuary, the place where I find comfort. I see you standing at the end of it, saying how you love to talk with me, our conversations stretching out as the sunlight slants through the windows.

Getting up, I head to your third-floor office, sit in your chair, and survey all your things, including your standing desk, willing you to come, summoning you to stand there once more. Then begins my struggle out of nightmares that sometimes consume both my days and nights.

Downstairs in the kitchen, I'm surrounded by all the many photos of you on the walls and propped on the counters as I try to make dinner for myself. Sometimes I haven't got the heart to cook anything, so I do what you often did: toast bread and pile it with peanut butter. But that only makes me feel your absence anew. It hits me how lonely it is to spend one winter evening after another and another alone, your face gazing at me, serious, smiling, sometimes with an expression of tranquil happiness, other times with a look that asks, "How did all this happen? Is this real?" These are the moods I see in our wedding photos. One snapshot pronounces, "I'm the king of the castle." Another insists, "Surely, I've reached nirvana, paradise, heaven." Take your pick.

"*Oh, darling!*" I'm still crying, and nine months have passed.

Now I think about Virginia Woolf's *Mrs Dalloway*. The poor woman, in menopause, believes it's all over for her. That, too, is how I feel, not because I'm in menopause but because I'm old, and having lost you, dear Gordon, feel life is all but over for me. Like Mrs Dalloway, metaphorically, I go up to the tower alone where the sheet is stretched tight and the bed narrow. Others are outside BlackBerrying in the sun — or today's equivalent. Woolf writes: "The door [to the tower] had shut, and there among the dust of fallen plaster and the litter of birds' nests how distant the view had looked, and the sounds came thin and chill …"

"Gordon! Gordon!" I cry out, just as Mrs Dalloway called to her husband. In her case, he came. You, my darling, can only appear when I remember you, when I summon you in thought, memory, dreams. And like Mrs Dalloway, I feel my share of life is sliced.

Is it only the skeleton of habit alone that upholds the human frame? But habit, routine, isn't something to be despised. Its joys are to be recognized and be grateful for because it's only when you're without it that you truly appreciate it. I wrote that on behalf of Spiros, one of my characters in *Helena*.

About Woolf's *Mrs Dalloway* again: I gave a formal review of it at the Faculty Club. One particular passage moved me profoundly, because I related to the woman who weeps for her beloved who's been dead for many centuries, so I read it aloud:

> Through all the ages — when the pavement was grass, when it was swamp, through the age of tusk and mammoth, through the age of silent sunrise … [she] stood singing of love — love which has lasted a million years … which prevails, and millions of years ago, her lover, who had been these centuries, had walked … but in the course of ages, long as summer days, and flaming, she remembered … that he had gone; death's enormous sickle had swept those tremendous hills, and when at last she laid her hoary

and immensely aged head on the earth … she implored the Gods to lay by her side a bunch of purple heather, there on her high burial place which the last rays of the last sun caressed; for then the pageant of the universe would be over.

That passage evokes All Souls' Day when dead lovers return. Oh, that you could return in some form, Gordon darling, be with me, look at me with those summer-blue eyes. And so yearning, I go to bed, curl up in a fetal position to find warmth and comfort, to cry for you, and for myself.

41

We Were Us

When inevitable regrets creep up on me — *I should have, could have, didn't do* — I remind myself of what I did do: I truly loved you, and you knew it. I added to your circle of friends, introduced you to concerts, operas, and plays, to a whole other life with many different people you would never have known. And then, together, we travelled to almost every place on earth. We walked. We dined. We made small talk among our discussions of literature and politics.

We were.

I'm still on Berkeley Street walking the aisles of No Frills as I've done all the numberless years, doing the same things in the same place, and suddenly how tired it all seems, how old I feel. I've been here, walked there, done this, and I'm doing it again and again, only now just for me — not us.

At this moment, I feel like a disembodied ghost — is there such a creature? — bleached through to my bones. I see myself naked, as though truthful to myself for the first time, I who always rushed to fix things up, not able to bear discord or anything not right. Immediately, I had to fix it. But I can't fix this.

We were *Us*. Such a heady concept in retrospect. In one sense, whether our experience with each other is, or was, good or bad, isn't important, only the sheer weight of it. Do either of us care about our sun-scarred skin, lines around eyes and mouth, the sagging skin, the bulging mid-line? No. You smile at me, and I at you, as if we're complicit in something that doesn't have to be defined.

And so I become preoccupied with the concept of *I* and *We*. It comes to me again and again when we're doing ordinary things, when we're at a party or any social occasion. It's the knowledge that you're there, that you're mine and I'm yours, that the enormity of what I've lost hits me.

I go out wherever and whenever I'm invited: to Victor Ostapchuk's dinner party, to a family occasion, to a movie group. I have no pleasure in any of it but go through the motions. Your absence stings, overwhelms. *Oh, Gordon! Gordon!*

42

Marriage, Grief

I often have thoughts about marriage, what it means in reality, in fantasy, and how it might play out for most people. Particular intimacy is its greater part, the knowledge that you're special to someone. Now I truly envy anyone having that other person with whom to share idle comments, gossip, thoughts about politics, the world, about everything. Not least, being cherished, being accepted the way you are.

Why did I feel throughout our marriage that our union was tenuous, even fragile? Not because we were unhappy — on the contrary! Perhaps it was because it was so wonderful, so perfect, a dream. Yes, it was like a dream from which I might awake any minute. Repeatedly, subconsciously, I ask myself: do I deserve this? And I suppose, after two previous failed marriages, I wonder if this one will last. All and none of these things. Don't take marriage for granted! Cherish it, and as I've said, polish it each morning and admire it in the evening. I feel in part that we've had two separate lives and only by accident have we come together. It might disappear any minute — as it has.

What comes to me often is the joy I felt in doing things for us: housework, making the bed, a meal, trimming the garden, sweeping the path to the street. Did I realize it at the time? Mostly yes. Seeing only one side of the bed rumpled reproaches me — only my clothes in the laundry. Sadness sweeps over me then, followed by dullness. Those mundane things we did unthinkingly I see now as beautiful interludes that enshrined our life together. Then I think that all the while elsewhere, people are fighting, sleeping, working, shopping …

What is beauty and where is it to be found? As Muriel Barbery says in *The Elegance of the Hedgehog*, "In great things that, like everything else, are doomed to die, or in small things that aspire to nothing, yet know how to set a jewel of infinity in a single moment?" Or as the Reverend Richard Fee said in his eulogy to you, Gordon, quoting Psalm 103:16, "As for man, his days are like grass, he flourishes like a flower of the field; the wind blows over it and it is gone."

The sense of *I* and *We* returns. I'm a speck flying solo, no anchor, no confidant. Even if a marriage isn't happy, I think, even if it limps along without the couple seeming to care about each other much anymore, still it's *We*, a unit, and each one in it will stand fast for the other if they have to.

As the weeks, months pass, the grey sterility of each morning awakening softens a little, but there remains the vision of a landscape ironed flat and featureless. Some days I can manage sufficiently well that I wonder, in fear, if I'm forgetting you. But today is an echo of others where I dwell on those things I should have known better, should have been nicer, warmer … and still I can't believe you're gone. Yesterday, while walking up Berkeley Street from Dundas as I've done countless times, I feel the magic of the street has gone. No nightingales sing anymore. No singing anywhere. Singing? And it comes back to me, that day in our house I walked about with songs on my lips. I heard you call out with joy in your voice, "No singing allowed in the house."

I laughed. "I don't call this singing."

Again, now what?

I pick up the collection of photos I printed of our many travels. One drops to the floor, and I pick it up. Oh, we're in Italy, in Florence. Why Florence? For the art, most of the world would say. For its history. Here is the stuff of storylines, of myth and magic, of legendary heroes and villains, all of it exuding an ancient history ...

"Another honeymoon?" we said almost in unison. "Okay!"

43

Florence

We're sitting in a Florentine garden in a pool of warm sunlight filtered through the leaves of lemon trees and mimosa. Our Airbnb, close to the heart of the city, is filled with perfumes, with birdsong and the hum of distant traffic. That first night we sit across a round table from each other, a bottle of Italian red wine between us, exhilarated by a sense that we've won a hefty lottery.

Florence, a city of opposites where the sublime and the terrible go hand in hand: da Vinci's notebooks and Machiavelli's *The Prince*. Dante's *Divine Comedy* and Boccaccio's *Decameron*. Savonarola's Bonfire of the Vanities and Botticelli's *The Birth of Venus*.

We tread the jagged, uneven streets and sidewalks — where there are any — sharing them with people, motorbikes, and cars. Walking here has its perils. The streets are so narrow that only small cars can traverse them, and many are repurposed as restaurants, as artists' studios. We saunter among blank and often ugly walls that tilt toward each other across narrow streets, walls with the accumulated grime of centuries. A door will open to reveal a tiny bar, a coffee shop, a restaurant, a quaint niche store selling upscale clothes, bags, jewellery. Or sweeping courtyards, gardens studded with sculptures, an old convent or monastery. One night, at a tiny corner shop that drapes itself about a jagged intersection of broken concrete, a bent, elderly man lugs crates of apples from the sidewalk into a tiny storage room, a place so small it's hard to imagine a living can be made from it.

As we stroll the streets of Florence, I feel I'm in the company of the sculptor Donatello, who walked here in scarlet robes, people saluting him, citizens making way for him. I wonder if the many sixteenth-century art workshops still exist and dream of finding one, of wandering into rooms and gardens full of sculptures and paintings.

Then there's Savonarola, an Italian monk and Christian preacher who was a reformer and martyr renowned for his clash with tyrannical Florentine rulers and a corrupt clergy. After the overthrow of the Medici in 1494, he became the sole leader of Florence, his apocalyptic rhetoric instilling fear in the hearts of his congregation. At the pulpit, he promised violent, imminent punishment for sinners while at the same time advocating for the faithful and the morally upright to endure the current period of tribulations. I shiver as I imagine myself in his congregation, his penetrating eyes fixed on me. Reward for the faithful would be a renewed golden age in Florence unlike any before — a Florence that would soon be transformed into the New Jerusalem. That was the dream.

I peer up at the face of Savonarola's sculpture in a piazza named after him. What riveting eyes he has, how piercing. With what genius the sculptor has shown the fanaticism and cruelty of the man! Those sinister eyes follow us as we move away. I wonder how many people he killed. The fear that must have pervaded the city is unimaginable.

Later, I recall how Sarah Dunant brought Savonarola to life in her historical novel *The Birth of Venus*, and we linger in the city's main square, the Piazza della Signoria, where the Bonfire of the Vanities took place near the Palazzo Vecchio, the town hall. "What a history! Such a history!" I keep exclaiming to you. Next, we move toward the fountain with a sculpted Neptune in dazzling white marble. Drawn by a chariot of four horses, Neptune is ringed by three young Tritons and four other figures.

All over again, I appreciate the riches of history, of myth, of fantasy that exist in this place.

We enter the Four Seasons Hotel, the chain's flagship and arguably the most magnificent in the world. It's also Canadian — hurrah! The eleven acres of gardens surrounding it are studded with bronze sculptures, pebbled walkways, shaped trees, and rose gardens.

Now, at last, I've seen some of the wealthy citizens' mansions and gardens and can imagine those days of Florence's Medici: a chapel somewhere in that Garden of Eden, a hired artist painting it with Gospel scenes and religious frescoes. Cosimo, Lorenzo — names out of books, men who enacted a bold, often violent history and left a legacy.

A more recent history is all about us: a black man from Kenya, well dressed, offers trinkets in return for euros. Some are aggressive. I wonder if they're economic or war refugees. It's hard to tell, but always unfortunate for them. As they leave a grocery store or any shop, most people hand such a beggar a few coins.

We're staying in a wonderful Airbnb on the city's outskirts, a place resembling a Matisse painting: two floors, a set of drums, a piano on the main floor, two bedrooms above reached by a curved staircase. When it's warm enough outdoors, we sit in a walled garden with mimosa climbing over those old stones, a bottle of Italian red wine on the round table between us. Fleetingly, I catch sight of two kittens racing each other in the garden.

"This is heaven," I say, meeting your shimmering eyes, see the lift in your shoulders, in your step when you get up. Travelling — truly, you're born to it. And you do it in your own inimitable way: relaxed, no timetables, little planning.

Each day in Florence, we make sure our route into the city centre takes us past the main doors of the Four Seasons. I think how perennially this is the world's top tourist destination, but how inconspicuous the street, how equally modest the door that opens to such an exalted place. We pause here each time we pass, trying to peer farther into it.

"Are we allowed to go in?" I ask a uniformed, youngish man outside the hotel.

"Of course," he replies. "Just walk in, have a coffee, walk around the grounds."

Whoa!: a Canadian accent, here at the doors of the world's greatest hotel. Well! We ask for his story and learn that he's an Alberta software programmer who became a ski bum — his words — on the slopes of Whistler Mountain.

"I met an Italian doctor," he says. "I married her, learned to speak Italian, and moved here. We've got a house in the Tuscany Hills. She's a pediatrician and commutes to hospitals in Florence, Siena, and Pisa. And here I am, doorman of a hotel."

His expression is one of self-deprecation, and we return his impish smile, shake his hand, and step into the fabled place.

Once through the main gates, we hover in the doorway of the hotel's palatial foyer, abashed and awed at its grandeur, at the stunning Renaissance palazzo renovated and preserved as a living museum. It's said that the hotel retains the building's magnificent original artwork, some of it more than five hundred years old.

We can't take our eyes off the marble statue of David, at the grandiosity of it, of all of it. Not having the courage to wander in farther, we return outdoors to begin an exploration of those eleven acres of statue-studded private gardens bequeathed to the city by Pope Leo XI.

"We should have stayed here!" I exclaim. "I bet there aren't many former papal residences you can sleep in."

"At $2,000, $3,000 a night?" you say. "Though you're worth it." You pick up your camera and repeatedly aim it at me.

In the central city, of one accord, we set out first to the Duomo, next to the Uffizi Gallery, then to the Galleria dell'Accademia, home to Michelangelo's *David*. You admire the engineering feat of Brunelleschi's famous dome, revered by architects and engineers worldwide. Together, we wander all over the city. We walk and walk, our steps in unison.

Each day is born in silvery splendour as though this magnificent city has infinite promises awaiting us. Our plan this day is to have what's called the Golden Dinner on Ponte Vecchio. Perhaps this is the world's most famous bridge, with its spectacular sunset vistas and a sweeping view of the River Arno and the tourist centre of the city itself.

I doubt anyone would argue against Florence being the great arts capital of Italy, especially since Michelangelo, Leonardo da Vinci, Botticelli, and Raphael "debuted" here.

"Florence claims to have more artistic treasures than any other square yard on earth," I tell you. "Astronomy, math …"

"A landlocked city with a non-navigational river, yet it produced explorers who mapped the New World," you finish for me.

Yes, Florence, a city that was the physical expression of the Renaissance and considered the cradle of Western civilization.

Again, we walk all over it, over the Ponte Vecchio many times back and forth. You especially enjoy knowing that this bridge was built in 1345. One afternoon, we climb the hill to the Boboli Gardens and are rewarded with fantastic views over the city.

Returning to the eleven acres of private gardens belonging to the Four Seasons Hotel, we happily get lost among numberless extraordinary statues dotted among a green expanse of lawn, trees, and flowering bushes.

The next day, I say, "But we have to see more than Florence. We're in Italy, after all." So off we go by bus to Siena, then Pisa.

"Are you going to climb this leaning structure?" I ask in Pisa. You hesitate, then decline. I don't ask why not. As we explore this city, what strikes us are the number of local families strolling in the dusk along the banks of the River Arno: parents, many children, and grandparents. It seems that the city streets are their playground, their garden, their place.

In the latter part of our stay, you're contacted about a job, and while it's an inconvenient time, you're pleased. I see it in your eyes, hear it in your voice, as I've heard it before.

44

New York City

Well, my dear heart, what do we do next but plan a trip to New York City.

Restless, one might comment, curious, adventure-seeking. Mostly, we look again for the exhilaration that comes from learning how other people live. Visiting museums. Traversing unfamiliar streets. And, of course, seeing for ourselves places famous the world over and that perhaps have other hidden treasures to discover.

We find a small flat on West Seventy-second Street, a two-minute walk from an entrance to Central Park called Strawberry Fields. Naturally, young men in 1960s costumes with guitars strum the Beatles' "Strawberry Fields Forever" all the days and evenings we're there. Enchanting — yes! We sit on benches in the park under a pale sun, then move among the throngs who flow around the edges of the park in counter-clockwise direction, all either walking or riding horses, biking, or rollerblading.

On our third day, I suggest we visit Washington Square. "It's magical," I tell you. "It keeps getting reinvented. It's full of history — and beautiful."

Washington Square's origins are humble. First, there was a period of violence, then this piece of land, acquired by the city, was used as a common burial ground, a potter's field. Public executions gave rise to the tale of the Hangman's Elm Tree in the northwest corner of the square. A military parade ground followed in 1826, a public park a year later.

Wealthy, prominent families who wanted to escape the disease and congestion of downtown Manhattan moved here eventually and built themselves elegant Greek Revival mansions on the square's north side. These are called The Row. With their Ionic and Doric columns and marble balustrades, they're considered among the finest Greek Revival dwellings in New York.

We arrive in the park and sit on a bench. I watch as your eyes rove all over it, appraising its dimensions and attributes: a ball court, a mini-restaurant and coffee bar, rose gardens, a shaded corner for chess. Washington Square reminds me of Henry James whose novel *Washington Square* was set on The Row. I fall into a reverie about James's novels, feeling again the intensity of his obsessions. Mentally, I revisit some of the themes that circle around his characters and their shenanigans, remember his depiction of the terrible condition of being unable to love.

Unable to love? Maybe to do so is a gift. I turn to gaze at you and think that to marry you and be with you are the easiest, and at the same time, the most profound things I've ever done. I reach up and rumple your hair as I so like to do. You give me that beautiful smile you keep for me, encircle me with an arm. In that moment, William

Wordsworth's lines on the French Revolution come to mind: "Bliss was it in that dawn to be alive, / But to be young was very heaven!"

Hey, we're in New York. We're not young, but we feel ourselves to be. We're young in our relationship. We linger here. We get up to ramble in the far corners of Manhattan: to the northernmost tip to find a medieval museum. To Harlem, to Soho, to Times Square, of course.

Not to be forgotten is the trip we make into Brooklyn where Graeme, my first husband, and I lived long ago. What a sea change from the 1970s. Eastern Parkway and it environs — the Botanic Gardens, the Brooklyn Museum, Park Slope, Prospect Heights, the public library, and not least, Prospect Park — have all been transformed, manicured, and cleaned up, yet remain beautiful.

45

How Our Things Outlast Us

I tell myself I shouldn't spend so much time with you in memory, Gordon, whether on holidays, at home, or with friends and family. I must stumble forward into a new, cruel reality — a life without you. Right now, I stretch out on our bed with a novel, intending to finish it in time for an upcoming book club discussion. But once more, I slide into the past, languidly watching patterns made by sunlight glancing through the leaves of the giant chestnut tree outside the window, my book face down on the counterpane. Next, I see you emerge from the shower, rummage through your sock drawer, then walk to my side of the bed to hug me. You bend to kiss me, then, suddenly, you're gone and nothing of you lingers. I remain there, staring at nothing. Life is a void.

Eventually, I go downstairs to make dinner, pretending to call out to tell you it's ready. Catching sight of the myriad photos of you on the kitchen walls, I tell myself I've been lucky, that I had a fabulous, joyous life with you. I think of all the travelling, all the little, everyday things that made me feel warm, secure, contented. I was happy! Did I know it? Some say happiness is only a memory. Some say it isn't any kind of achievement but the path to it.

For distraction, I go wherever I'm invited. I return invitations. When I'm entertaining, you're sitting beside me on the living room couch, or at one end of the dining table, or in the sunroom. I feel the burden of being just me, that I'm not enough. With you, I might be at work in the kitchen, in the dining room, happily leaving you to entertain our guests. I'll hear you from the kitchen, talking, laughing.

I begin to use the elliptical machine again, taking George Eliot's *Middlemarch* on my Kindle to read while I exercise. Afterward, I sit in your empty chair and fill my eyes with images of you, of all the accoutrements you left behind. Your pajama pants and a pair of shorts hang over the railing, a pair of running shoes on the floor beneath. Above, a sweatband and water bottle. I remember hearing your laugh echoing down the stairs as you listened to a podcast when exercising. But today, my images of you for the first time seem blurred, faded, as though part of your spirit has finally risen and vacated this space once so filled with you. Am I imagining it because I've been dreading this? I just know that something feels different, emptied out and faded, like an old colour photo with its edges ragged.

How our things outlast us, how much they refer to us. Your feet have warmed those running shoes. That sweatband held your curly grey hair. Your sweatshirt and all your clothes remain with your imprint, with a sort of ghostly animation. Once the looking glass, too, reflected your face smiling, frowning. "Who's that old man staring back at me?" you'd say, peering quizzically at me, one eyebrow raised. The empty door, your empty chair, flash in my mind suddenly as though with your silhouette, then it's gone.

Frantically, I try to call you back. I will myself to see your blue eyes gazing at me, the familiar smile in them. I remain in your chair. I must get up, be busy, so I arrange events and visits. A week, a few weeks, a month go by crowded with meetings with friends, with members of my writers' group, my Oakville family, with Graeme, my first husband.

One morning, I read a personal essay in the *Globe and Mail* about a woman trying to cope with the death of her husband. It activates all my own sadness, and that night I dream you're standing in the doorway of our bedroom, beginning to enter, only to start backing away.

"It's okay," I say. "I'm still awake. You can come in."

But you don't.

And I remember you're dead. I look again, and this time, see you in the doorway to my office leaning against the door frame. You smile, talk, move from one side of the door frame to the other, all the while speaking. Then again, you're back in the doorway to our bedroom.

Now you're not.

Just empty doors — *I will meet you at the empty door …*

"I don't need to work," you told me from time to time. "I might retire."

You never do, and I understand. Although in your seventies and financially needing no income derived from working, when mining companies from around the world come searching for you and your singular expertise, you feel wanted, necessary, part of the everyday working world. You accept all the projects offered. And so, in my mind, you're still up there in your third-floor office.

46

Learn Something New, Walk a Path from Yesterday

In a room full of people, you lean toward me as I speak, your eyes lingering on me, and suddenly we're the only ones in the room, in the whole world. You come upon me in the hallway, your eyes alight on mine, and spontaneously, effortlessly, you pick me up and hoist me in the air, laughing at my seeming weightlessness.

Now you're standing by my side of our bed and smiling down at me. Another time you catch sight of a photo of a woman in a magazine and say with delight in your voice, "She looks like you, don't you think?"

No. She looks very ordinary. She has an okay face, nothing special, and flat brown hair. But you insist, and because it gives you pleasure, I nod.

One late September evening, we're at an anniversary dinner for graduates of the University of Toronto's Faculty of Engineering, those who have made it from the 1940s into the 2000s, all seated at tables according to the decade in which each graduated. I get up and walk around the room, marvelling, and at the same time sad, at the ravages time has wrought in the faces and bodies of the older graduates.

One day, I'm at Service Ontario to replace my driver's licence, having had my purse stolen. I've been there all morning. I turn from the counter to walk toward the exit when I catch sight of you propped against the back wall. You give me that special melting, quizzical smile you keep just for me, and a bolt of joy shoots into my heart. I've only been gone two or three hours, yet you came looking for me. I fly to you, laugh and hug you.

"Sweetie, what are you doing in this place?" I ask.

"Just wandering in the area and thought you might still be here."

Hand in hand, we go in search of a replacement purse for me, then somewhere for lunch.

Dinner parties are sometimes a little fraught for me when I realize you have little experience in what a host's duties are.

"Um, sweetie, could you try to remember to refill our guests' wineglasses?" I ask, but inevitably will have to keep prompting. "And do remember to get everyone a chair." What I don't say, but feel tempted to, is: "Don't drop into the most comfortable one and leave a guest standing."

I think about these little things, and in my older, more accepting age, ask myself: "Has the theory of the solar system been advanced by graceful manners and a certain type of etiquette?" Then I recall what you said during your wedding speech, that "I'm Carolyn's third husband, and I'm the lucky one."

Lucky? Just maturity, I think. Maybe people shouldn't marry until they're old.

"I just love you so much," I say to you across the table, or in bed before sleeping, and again while you sit watching television.

"Likewise," you say. How long does it take you to say, "I love you, too"? Maybe a year, maybe two? How long before you can more freely express your emotions? Another year passes before you say things like "I was proud of you." That came after I entertained your boss at a formal dinner and made him laugh. Once, after a library talk that was successful, you said, "That went well."

How easily we settle into comforting habits that over time wear into reassuring grooves. We become each other's constant with little effort required to make it all work, just a little compromise here and there.

How do we keep the glow, the sense of unending discovery alive once we've pledged ourselves to familiarity? How might we be enchanted by discovery's opposite, routine, and find in constancy a stimulation as rich as novelty provides? It's said that the story of every marriage is perhaps the story of what happens after the endless summer. *learn something new, walk a path from yesterday.*

The most memorable for us is our ability to do the ordinary, to take care of everyday things, to keep working, going to the office, in your case, to the third floor. To look after our extended families and be neighbourly. Nothing lasts. No! We must take nothing for granted. *Carpe diem.*

I marvel when I think about you, curious how you were in your young life. How many times do we lament that we've known each other only in our later life when youth and middle age have already passed? But did you deliberately go out to make a difference in life, to shape your own path during your stint upon life's stage? Whether consciously or otherwise, certainly you weren't "shapen after the average and fit to be packed by the gross," as George Eliot writes in *Middlemarch.*

I remember comments by two of your colleagues: "Gordon was unique" and "Gordon was ... different."

Something else, *Middlemarch* again, adapted somewhat by me for you: *It was not for you to walk like a ghost in its old home and make the new furniture ghastly.*

This is also who you are and were.

The man and husband who, early in our relationship, comes with me and my two small granddaughters to a swimming pool in Toronto's

Beach. Who gets in the water and gently, patiently, persuades the terrified younger one to get in and get wet.

The man and husband who travels with my son and family when they move from Toronto to Kelowna and on to the Lake Country in British Columbia. Imagining they'll have a difficult journey, my son driving the truck with all their worldly possessions, Anita in the car with a small daughter in the back. You join them, helping with the driving, with unloading, then you fly home.

And this: "Can you bear to come with me to dig up some dirt?" I ask one day.

"Dirt on who?"

"No, silly. Dirt — topsoil for the garden. The city's giving it away for free, but you have to get it yourself." And there you are alongside me in the wasteland that is the old Portlands, digging buckets of the stuff until we can't carry any more.

And this: one day I drop into the Freedom Mobile kiosk to get an attachment fixed on my phone. You once took me there to purchase the phone and told me if I ever needed help to go there and ask for Noreen.

I do. "I'm Gordon Watts's wife," I tell her.

"Gordon Watts? Oh!" Her eyes light up. "He's a real sweetie." Wow! She singled you out among the hundreds who come to her every day.

Nights for us are as in this excerpt from one of Pablo Neruda's *One Hundred Love Sonnets*:

> I love you like this because I know no other way to love,
> only in this way in which I am not and you are not,
> so close that your hand upon my chest is mine,
> so close that your eyes close with my sleep.

47

Berkeley Street and Family

How long is it okay to mourn you so deeply? Gordon darling, I miss you fiercely and sometimes don't know how I can do this. I feel so alone. Especially coming home and when entering the front door or the back door from the garage, I expect you to be waiting for me there. It was lovely, the thought of you, to talk to you, be with you, to love you.

Still, I roam the streets looking for you. When anyone comes toward me with a vague resemblance to you, my heart stops. Grief, fierce and piercing, sweeps over me because it's not you. It never can be you, and I'm diminished, demolished. I long to see you look at me just one more time, one last time ... just open your eyes, open your eyes and look at me — please!

Your family, too, Gordon, misses you terribly, especially Mary, who continues to feel your death as an abandonment of her, of us, and that the family has drifted apart and become fractured.

I tell her it's we who have changed. We've actually cohered, and I remind her how fourth sibling, Robert, regularly phones us. Murray and Robert talk on the phone. Matt comes to more family functions, and David's children to them all. David is always in contact. I think again about your siblings, Gordon: how David loves to drop in. Mary still cries for you and always wanted you to herself for a little while, each of you sharing similar views of the world. And how you loved to talk to your brother-in-law, Peter! Then there's Mimi, fifth sibling. She tells me she loved your guidance, your sense of humour, your love of her baking, your "nerd" talks. She remembers you driving her ten-year-old self to ballet classes in an orange MG and asking her to change the gears with her left hand.

Then again, Robert, who comes from Calgary to trod the streets where you walked, to see what you saw, to trace the paths you took. What love! And Murray: he phoned you every few weeks. You signalled me who was calling to let me know you'd be tied up for an hour or two.

All of them still cry for you.

"You and Gordon were so tight together," Mary tells me, and I understand what getting together with me withdrew from her. Far back in time when I still lived in the Distillery condo, she came to visit, to stand beside you, put her arm through yours, and said, "Don't we look alike?" Not really, so I suppose she was inferring another kind of kinship. She also knew you were intellectual equals.

"Gordon was awkward, gawky, and nerdy when young," she tells me now. "He drifted from place to place in small apartments, always messy." She was implying you had no real home. And the day she stood in our Berkeley Street Victorian house we so lovingly decorated, she turned to me and said, "Gordon had nothing, and now he's got you — and he's got all this."

I tell her I'm so sorry that I never had a chance to meet her mother — your mother — whom you all loved dearly. She died six months before I met you, Gordon, and she was your first and greatest love.

Sometimes I wipe my eyes and marvel at what you and I achieved. Is it real? How has it happened? What have I done to deserve this prolonged honeymoon on Berkeley Street, interrupted only by yet more travel? Yes, travel: it seems we really can't help ourselves.

48

Britain

Oh, to be in England — well, in all or any part of Britain. "This sceptred isle … this other Eden," as William Shakespeare says in *Richard II*, is, to an earlier generation of New Zealanders, their real home. I've travelled here many times to visit friends, to tour with relatives from

Down Under, and simply to wander it. Images flit of verdant pastures and dripping yew trees, of ancient stones in crooked churchyards and the maw of darkened battlegrounds, of cities with blackened walls. And here is London, its streets weighted with names invoking fame, myth, and history, of boulevards strewn with jerky streams of people.

"I want you to meet my friends," I tell you, Gordon, and reach up to straighten your shirt collar. Today, you're wearing one of your several flowered blue-print shirts that deepens the blue of your eyes. I run my fingers through your flattened hair. "You're an arresting-looking fellow," I say. "I'd chase after you at first glimpse, but you look even more interesting with your hair piled up — like this."

"How about we travel all over, as well?" you answer to the suggestion we meet my friends. "Take a train all the way up the east coast and back down the west and meet your friends in between."

This is exactly what we do. What an exuberant ride about this land with its thousands of years of history, with its kings and queens and wars, its Roman ruins, its cathedrals, castles, and rings of ancient stones. But where to begin and where to stop a while at night? And what beds await us?

From London, we travel to the walled city of York, founded by the ancient Romans, with its York Minster Gothic cathedral. Arriving late in the day, we miss an exhibition that traces the life of fifteenth-century Plantagenet King Richard III. I'm enamoured of the story about this unfortunate king who, according to Shakespeare, murdered his nephews, the princes, in the Tower of London. But apparently, recent research shows that he might not have. (Shakespeare had Elizabeth I to consider when writing *Richard III*.)

Now we're in Scotland on a bus tour of Glasgow. Then in Inverness, the largest city and cultural capital of the Highlands, built where the River Ness meets the Moray Firth. The city was made famous by Diana Gabaldon's novel and television series *Outlander*.

I do relate to remote, brooding places, though this isn't necessarily how the city is or how it feels about itself. But it is windswept and cold. I shiver — well, it's only April, after all. In an open main square where the bus leaves us, you take off your zippered grey jacket and put it around my shoulders.

That first day, we tour Inverness's Old Town indoor markets, its cathedral, and the eighteenth-century Old High Church. The next day, we're in a museum that traces Highland history.

The most memorable thing is to come: an evening walk as darkness falls, the night already black. For a while, we follow the River Ness, struck by the blackness of the water running below blackened concrete steps that lead down to it, by the blackened stones of the cathedral, and indeed, by all the blackened buildings. Then, cold, shivering, we see light spilling out of a half-open door to a restaurant, riotous life within it.

"Look!" I grab your arm. Peering in the doorway, we see women in swirling skirts and stiletto heels dancing in the arms of suit-clad men. Neon lights pierce through the gloom to illuminate tables laden with discarded food and empty wine and beer bottles.

"All this elegance in such a black place," I say, awed. "I guess they're compensating for their cold, dark outdoor world."

Then comes a tour of Culloden Field. How impossible to imagine what happened here, and on such a bare, ordinary stretch of scrubby, flat land. "How many Scots Highlanders died?" I ask.

"About two thousand, I think," you say. A low wind moans over bristled grass and bracken, nothing to relieve the landscape's emptiness. But bloody images insist on intruding, and I turn my back on this infamous field.

You want to visit Fort William, but it's too early in the year and the fort remains closed, so instead we travel west and south to Glasgow, then pause in Chester. Our beds that night, as in our Waiheke Island sojourn in New Zealand, are up a ladder disguised as a staircase. Up and up we climb, you protecting your head, to reach a tiny space with two single beds, dark-stained ceiling crossbeams directly above our heads. But exhausted, we sleep the dreamless sleep of unthreatened monarchs — if there ever were such creatures.

The next day, we run along the old stone walls that surround the city and come to a statue of King Charles I, his staff raised, his flag blowing in the breeze.

"Treason," I say. "That's what they accused him of back then. He believed he ruled by divine right, like all monarchs then. He defied

Parliament and fought the armies of his English and Scottish parliamentarian enemies in what's called the English Civil Wars."

"And after his defeat, he was beheaded," you finish for me.

As we peer over the walls and into the back gardens of the little houses, I wonder how it might feel to live up against those ancient walls, the figure of King Charles I a constant reminder of their bloody history. I guess those who do no longer see, or notice, that such history even occurred.

While touring the art galleries along a main street, we find a Fat Lady painting. You want it, determined to get a copy somewhere, somehow. We never do, but not for lack of trying. Later, you find a copycat Fat Lady painting in Mexico and bring it home. Do I know you, this mathematical man and engineer who must have a Fat Lady?

Chester — what ancient beauty. What history, not least the Olde King's Head Pub dating from the 1600s — very atmospheric. Afterward, and once outside, you hike one way along the old city walls, I another, meeting up to watch a group of uniformed schoolgirls playing on the green fields below us. Again, I wonder if anyone currently living here ever feels the weight of history, and I'm back to King Charles I and what he stood and fought for. What would have been their history if he'd defeated Parliament and civil war hadn't ensued?

Ah, the what-if's of life: what if I never met you, Gordon?

• • •

We're in the British Museum in London. I marvel at the intensity of your concentration, your absorption, particularly with the Roman period in Britain. But everything in the museum absorbs you, and I see you again standing with your head bent, studying dates, proportions, events, while I animate the inanimate.

We have many triumphal walks around parts of London and through its famous parks and museums, its streets, including Carnaby, Pudding Lane, Oxford, Petticoat Lane. We explore its ancient cathedrals, its churches, particularly one by Nicholas Hawksmoor, an architect studying under Sir Christopher Wren, made notorious in the novel *Hawksmoor* by Peter Ackroyd.

I know you to have an urgent impulse for exertion, for motion, especially walking, as though your forward movement is an aphrodisiac. And I see you stride wide-open roads, glimpse you on city streets with their noise and clamour, around where we live, among what is sometimes a freak show. In frigid winters, you travel the downtown streets without hat, gloves, or scarf. Freedom: you love it, that sense of stepping purposefully through life. I know it as one of your passions. Another thought comes to me: that your mind is probably not on passing scenery but on the cosmos, on abstract concepts and theories of the universe.

49

A Nightingale Sings

In the month we spend in London in Wapping in a wonderful bed and breakfast, we make the twenty-minute walk twice a day to the underground station at Aldgate East and back. We come to know those streets as well as our own, and soon feel as if this is our home and where we belong. On our way "home," we linger by coffee shops, bakeries, a delicatessen, an occasional boarded-up shop. At night, I don't bother to lower the window shades since we look out over railway tracks at some distance; nobody to see me as I undress, but passengers flying by in a railway carriage.

"Who would want to see?" I ask you. "I love this place!"

Our London home is roomy, with two large bedrooms, two bathrooms, and an enormous living room. Right beside the bed and breakfast is Wilton's Music Hall, while an ivy-covered church sits opposite, foxes howling outside it in the night. Our joy in each other is magnified in this place, in this extraordinary city. Within a twenty-five-minute walk, we're at the Tower of London and Tower Bridge. How many times do we go across that bridge to the south side of the River Thames to lean over the railings and dream about the life that's sailed upon it to all corners of the earth?

And then there's Berkeley Square and a nightingale! Ah, my beloved, when you turn and smile at me, when I'm with you, nightingales sing the sweetest of melodies day and night. I remember the drinks we had with your colleague, Graham Clow, at the Mayfair Hotel, close to Berkeley Square, recalling how we grasped goblets filled with dark red wine in a room shaded by blood-red drapes. At those recollections, the euphoria I felt while watching the world slide by beyond the portals of that noble establishment returns, the world as it must have been two hundred years before: carriages drawing up, liveried footmen bowing, elegant women sweeping up their skirts.

The words of the famous song come back to me:

I may be right, I may be wrong
But I'm perfectly willing to swear
That when you turned and smiled at me
A nightingale sang in Berkeley Square.

Berkeley Square lives in my dreams, this oval-shaped public garden in Mayfair in London's West End. Even in the dusk as we stumble upon it, I see outlines of its famous plane trees, even perhaps one of the Great Trees of London, said to be the most valuable street tree in Britain. Now, adjusting to the dim light, I make out the park's central fountain and some of its statues. I long to go on a hunt for the legendary sculpture of the dancing hares, but it's dark and we've got no time. We have a concert at St. George's Church in Hanover Square to attend.

Drunk now on the beauty of the park, even more on the thought of a nightingale there, I sing aloud the words of the song until we arrive at St. George's Church where steaming glasses of mulled wine are put into our outstretched hands. The night has barely begun. Through the venerable old church door, we're ushered in, then more glasses of hot mulled wine are placed in our hands.

What a night to cherish as one of the best, the finest, most memorable of all the nights we lived and loved those few short years together. The choir, the audience, how heartily, lustily, we sing "The Twelve Days of Christmas." And afterward, with our friends and their friends and all the noise of us, we fill up a pub across the street with laughing, talking, and shared experiences. With riposte, jokes, wit, and confessions, we remain until it closes. Drunk, laughing, happy with ourselves as though we've achieved something unique, have robed ourselves in a rare kind of happiness — some conceit, I suppose — clumsily, we navigate our way on the Underground. Then comes the longish walk to our bed and breakfast — the mystery of how we get there never solved.

But we're not finished yet with touring, and another highlight is the south coast of England with a visit to my long-time friend, Gemma Hooper. It's here that I learn something else about you, Gordon. In Chichester, we visit a pub where a guitarist plays and sings folk songs. I can't fathom what's in his voice, his rendering of English folk songs, but you love it, speak of it often and fervently, you who have been described by your son as not hearing music, that zeroes and ones are enough for you. You bring up that song in the pub frequently, long after we return from England. There must have been a note, a tone, or a melody that evoked a poignant, long-ago memory.

We wander this small town and tour its almshouse. The term *almshouse* isn't familiar to us, so we're curious.

The buildings date to the end of the thirteenth century and have twenty-nine flats surrounded by large, beautiful walled gardens. Apparently, almshouses have existed for more than a thousand years and have enabled people in need to retain their independence and continue to live in their communities. To be eligible, one must be elderly, of limited financial means, of good character, and in sufficiently good health to cook and housekeep for themselves. They must have resided for not fewer than five years in an ecclesiastical parish in the Diocese of Chichester or any part within fifteen miles of the Cathedral Church of the Holy Trinity.

Chichester is a charming place of about twenty-six thousand people, the only city in West Sussex, and one with a long history of settlement in both Roman and Anglo-Saxon times. Old? Indeed, its cathedral dates to the eleventh century.

Gemma drives us to her son's home where we're entertained by him, his wife, and two sons. In their large sunlit garden are the remnants of an old stone wall that the family intends to remove.

"Oh, no!" I exclaim. "I love stone walls! Maybe we can have it shipped back to Canada?"

"I can build you a stone wall," you say.

After that, we wander through a woodland carpeted with bluebells. Gemma points out the difference between English and North American types, and of course for her, the English bluebells are superior. Crickets, a light rain, moss beneath our feet — these are the details I recall. Then on we go to explore old Roman ruins. New houses have been built over the spas and remnants of Roman homes. Again, I wonder what it would feel like to do that, to be atop people who lived their lives there thousands of years earlier. A bit creepy, I think.

Gemma comes with us to Salisbury, an ancient city with a cathedral made famous anew by Edward Rutherfurd in his novel *Sarum*. History is marked all about us. Dark waters beckon, and we walk a path alongside the river past stone walls and beneath the old city gate, which still today is ceremoniously closed at a certain time each night. I dream of living in the apartment above that city gate, which is advertised for rent, imagining myself sitting at the wide window directly above it and pretending I live in those earlier days.

"Hey, we could rent it and live here for part of the year," I tell you.

"Sure, if you want," you say at once.

A light rain begins to fall, but we don't care, and we sit in an outdoor café listening to evensong filtering through the stained-glass windows of the cathedral.

50

London

Returning to London, we spend an evening with John Hooper and his wife, Julia, at their home in Clapham, South London. We get off at the wrong Underground stop because you insist, but I've been there before and know. I want to tease and tell you you're not always right, but refrain. The early dusk is beautiful, and we set out to walk the long distance to the previous station and to Almeric Road. I'm euphoric about the velvety early evening, at the particular softness in the air, at the grassy slopes, the gardens, the plane trees of Clapham Common. Not least, elegant Georgian, Victorian, and Edwardian houses overlooking the streets and the park. As on that sloping road on Waiheke Island, I want to shout, "I'm alive. I'm young and alive and in love."

We're late! I tell our hosts that we've already had our tour, so briefly we walk among merchants' shops on Northcote Road, a place where I've shopped many times before. I could return there anytime in a heartbeat. It's a place where one can wander into many varied specialty stores: a cheese shop, a wine store, a butcher's shop, where the proprietor regales you with local and world gossip and has opinions and a philosophy on every subject you care to raise with him. Other shoppers invariably join in. Oh, to have a community life like that!

And then comes the pub crawl one evening along the River Thames from Wapping on the north shore with John and Julia, the latter our guide. Is there anyone anywhere who doesn't know the tales of this mighty waterway, wide with twisting currents and landing stages all along its banks, studded with large and small vessels heading upstream or out toward the ocean, upon whose waters kings, queens, and princes have sailed on down through the ages, which carried prisoners to the Tower of London, explorers to remote parts of the earth, and pleasure boats to other destinations? Those banks, those currents, if they could speak, would tell of the rich and the fallen, the mighty and the destitute. "What greatness had not floated on the ebb of that river," writes Joseph Conrad in *Heart of Darkness*.

We have a drink in each pub, including Ramsgate, the Captain Kidd, and The Grapes, the last in Limehouse on Narrow Street and where Charles Dickens wrote on the third floor and actor Sir Ian McKellen is currently co-owner. Soon, we're lightheaded, happy, and very pleased with ourselves.

On arriving back in Toronto, I reflect on the people I introduced you to in Britain, Gordon: John and Julia, Gemma, and my dear, long-time friends, Steve and Bev Howe in Cardiff. You and I travelled there by train to southern Wales, arriving to stay for a bank holiday weekend. Those three days saw a house full of laughing, chattering adults and their children and grandchildren. I swear that if love fills and expands a house, surely, theirs would have lifted off somewhere into the stratosphere.

51

Illness and Surgery

I'm coming up to the last year or so of your life, Gordon, searching for signs or presentiments of what's to come. But I don't know exactly what I'm looking for.

Your end almost does come when you have prostate surgery in February 2018 and everything that can go wrong does. With stubbornness you're affectionately known for, and against my and your brother's advice, you choose to have the surgery performed at East General Hospital, now called Michael Garron. I ask why you won't go to Toronto General where David was operated on so successfully. My question is echoed by your brother.

You answer only that you like your surgeon and don't discuss it further — this is the unknowable you. But I understand you've had sixty something years during which you've made your own decisions without the habit of consulting anyone else. Any input from me about your surgery won't change your mind.

Your near-death experience begins right after the surgery, with many complications. Afterward, interminably, we walk those narrow hospital corridors — more empty corridors! — you holding your catheter bag, I pushing the IV pole up and down, again and again. Your friend, Lee Barker, visits twice, doesn't like the look of you, and talks to the attending nurse. You're discharged home but don't do well. The following day, you've got a fever. Alarm bells! Visiting family members comment that you seem ill. You even confess that you don't feel well.

Your discharge instructions are that if you have a fever, you're to return to the hospital at once. I call an ambulance, and because of a severe ice storm that leaves layers of treacherous white stuff on streets and sidewalks, I ask to have you taken to Toronto General.

How many hours, a day, two, do you lie in the emergency room, only to come close to dying right there? I sit with you during one of those emergency-room visits. Lying on the stretcher beside you, my cheek against yours, I run my hands through your hair and whisper to you but feel you're not here, not there, and suddenly I sense you sliding away. In panic, I jump up and look for your emergency nurse.

Calm, unhurried, the nurse looks at me. "Is he worse than when he came here?"

"Yes, yes, he is! Look, I'm not a hysterical kind of person, but he's definitely worse. He needs a doctor — like now!"

After what seems like hours but is perhaps fifteen minutes, a doctor comes, assesses you, and without fuss, orders you admitted upstairs to a ward. It's the middle of the night. After untold hours there with your faithful brother, David, beside me, he persuades me to go home and drives me there. The next morning, I'm told you're a little better and can be discharged home. I'm confused, doubtful, but race off to pick you up. I arrive to find an attending physician about to sign the discharge papers. She stops, stands for long minutes peering at you, then returns to flipping through your chart.

"Something's not right here," she finally says, continuing to shuffle through the pages. "I'm sending you upstairs to have your lungs scanned." Then she gives orders and leaves.

You're diagnosed with multiple pulmonary emboli — blood clots in the lungs! Not to speak of torn stitches and a large abdominal hematoma. Again, you're admitted upstairs. David sits with me throughout the night and during the following day. What a faithful brother! At some point, Mary and sister-in-law, Tanya, join me.

The next morning, you're to be discharged, but I refuse to take you home because you still have an intermittent fever. The only bed found for you is in the transplant ward. What a beautiful oasis this is with plants, flowers, and shining empty spaces, not like any hospital ward I've ever seen.

The nurse admitting you studies the long, lean form of you prostrate on the stretcher, clears her throat, and says, "I've got to weigh you, so how do you ... er ... perambulate?"

"I put one foot in front of the other."

I laugh. You're going to be okay.

What a long haul back to health for you. Pulmonary embolism is an extremely serious complication on top of all the others, and I remain worried. It's also a rather cranky patient I have at home for a while, but then you get up, get going, and resume old routines.

By late summer, you're largely well, and we visit my daughter and son-in-law in their townhouse in Ellicottville in Upstate New York. We very much enjoy being with them in that picturesque little place. Largely in ski country, the town comes alive in summer during long weekends. You're able to walk with me all over it, to sit with me on its main street for coffee and lunch. Both of us spend a lot of time in its small memorial library where there are always books for sale and invariably we come back with armfuls. Books, glorious books!

In October, we fly to Kelowna in British Columbia, then on to the Lake Country in the province to see the beautiful home of my son, Paul, and daughter-in-law, Anna, on a hill overlooking Wood Lake and the Okanagan Valley. You seem well. You love my family, and they adore you.

I recall the memorable summer we spent with them at Tofino on the west coast of Vancouver Island, their favourite holiday resort. Wanting to give us a special holiday, they book us a log cabin with a hot tub under the stars, also an afternoon at a spa, one of us to have a facial, the other a massage.

"I don't want a massage," you said, and I laughed at the image of you having one. By default, you had the facial. I remember the two of us side by side in fluffy wraparound dressing gowns, our feet in aromatic water as we ate rabbit food.

When we leave their home and the Lake Country, my daughter-in-law, on behalf of her then seven-year-old daughter, Lindsay, gives you a card that says:

> Gordon, when I look at you, I wonder so about where you've been living all those many years on earth, and about all you know

within. You smile that very secret smile and I know you know so much. But you just look at me with love and share your gentle touch. Thank you just for being there, for showing me how life is lived. You teach me in everything you do, and all you have to give. God bless you for your faithfulness, by arriving where you are — so true. Thanks for being you. I love you.

This small, special-needs daughter mostly shuns close contact with adults but creeps up to you, sits on your lap, allows you to pick her up and throw her into the air. She loves and trusts you.

My son says this of you: "I haven't seen my mother so happy in a long time. When we see her and Gordon together, our hearts feel lighter and the world seems brighter because their love and happiness are contagious."

The Lake Country also means vineyards. Wine tasting is Paul's particular interest, so we trek all over this beautiful but sparsely populated part of British Columbia. We're not wine connoisseurs but feel, for his sake, we must pay homage to Dionysus. And, indeed, as we drive up Mission Hill, the giant clock tower strikes a half-hour, and in my imagination, its tolling is the summoning of the faithful to gather. A solemnity bordering on the religious is in the air, and I suppose for some, wine and wine-tasting are just that — a religion. I lean against a railing admiring the great sweep of gardens falling away down the slope to the lake below. Intoxicated with the scene, I muse to you that most people enjoy a variety of landscapes, and I, diehard city person that I am, can imagine spending a chunk of time here.

"Yes, sure," you say.

"We could rent our house and come here for a couple of months each year. What do you think?"

"Sure," you repeat, but in a tone that prompts me to turn and consider you. It's a stranger standing beside me! Such is our togetherness that I assume you're there always beside me.

• • •

My thoughts wander over the many large gatherings we've enjoyed at Christmas and New Year's with our families — mine, yours, ours.

My Oakville family loves you. My first husband, his wife, and family like and respect you. My daughter says you're a wonderful addition to our family, and my son-in-law, Jim, with tears in his eyes at your deathbed says, "But he was such a nice man!" Granddaughter Rachel relates how you understood her, and Cameron, how much she'll miss you. I remember that each time I plan a visit to our family in Oakville, Jim hopes you'll be with me, and when together, the two of you will immediately fall into high-level discussions of politics, political figures, television programs, and talk shows.

52

A Last Return to New Zealand

In February 2019, we're on our way for yet another visit to New Zealand, this time for just three weeks. We're not to know it will be our last trip together, not just here, but anywhere.

We realize we've covered quite a chunk of the country, but there's still much more to see. As well, one could revisit this idyllic isle numberless times and never exhaust its beauty.

This time we plan an adventure with my sisters and their spouses on the Coromandel Peninsula. To Kiwis, the very name conjures images of a magical place, of a geography that's everything a big city isn't: a mountainous interior clad in rainforest. Endless white sand beaches. Few people — in fact, a virgin world. We trek through untouched bush from one lonely beach to another, and here you are again, Gordon, feeling the sand between your toes, your head at an angle as though listening for birds unfamiliar to you: fantails, kingfishers, tūī, and bellbirds.

You and I often wander off to check out the tiny town and its one main street. I come across the public library, and you, to your astonishment, discover a shop filled with rock and mineral collections from all over the world. Rocks. Minerals. That's what you know. It's hard to get you out of there, and also the library.

53

At Home

It's the end of March and we're back in Toronto. At some point, I become aware that I seem to be going out a lot to various clubs and groups: two writers' groups, two book clubs, CSARN. This last is the hub that brings together older artists from different communities to share ideas, concerns, and information, linking "the silos" and creating its own unique community. Vaguely, I feel my going out is leaving you at home too much. How much is too much? How much togetherness does a couple need or want? Are we two people? Sometimes I think we're one.

My particular joy is to come home and entertain you, regale you with stories about the people I've seen and all that I've done. At night, if I've been out in the car, I'll park it in the garage at the end of our garden, see the bright splash of light spilling across the patio from the sunroom, and run up the steps to you. You've already thrown open the door. There you are in your chair before the television, bathed in light and smiling up at me. How I love that!

One current preoccupation is that I've written another novel, this one called *Phantom Siblings*. I finished it a year ago and have been trying to find a publisher for it, all the while knowing I've got little chance of finding one. When discouraged, I console myself by remembering George Eliot's line in *Middlemarch*: "Failure after long perseverance is much grander than never to have a striving good enough to be called a failure."

One thing I do notice about you, my beloved, is that you seem more security-conscious. You order cameras for the outside of our house, buy rods to insert to secure both sliding glass door upstairs and down. You won't allow me to leave the house even for a minute without activating the house alarm. It's been said that after major surgery a person might feel they've been invaded. Perhaps this explains it, perhaps it's an exaggeration of how you've always been.

April blusters in and blows out. We enjoy dinners with friends, a classical concert at Roy Thomson Hall …

May arrives, cool, often wet — a late spring. I go to the local plant nursery, anyway. I meet my neighbour, Greg, there. He buys me a huge basket of flowers. I thank him and we chat. I tell him I can't imagine not being alive, that life is a joy and there's so much to look forward to. When I get home, I find you in your sunroom chair smiling up at me. "So did you buy out the nursery?"

"Oh, maybe about half," I reply.

My diary tells me we toured the Art Gallery of Ontario with friends, visited my daughter and family in Oakville. We see your son, Matt, here and there.

One evening, I set up a dinner party for two couples. On another, I purchase tickets for a jazz concert. But then I lose the address and can't find the venue. On May 11, we go to a Beethoven concert with another couple. On Sunday, we have afternoon tea with other friends. Thursday, May 16, we're at our monthly book club at the Faculty Club, but I don't remember the book we discussed. I think you might have decided not to go since you didn't have time to read it.

Then, suddenly, our life together, a life that seemed to have just begun, stopped. You died. Nothing else changed, and my life would wind its way on without you. No answering words, not even an echo. All must begin again, with the light all but blotted out. Perhaps the sun might shine again someday for me, but never as brightly.

When you die, my grief begins as a ribbon of dread that mounts slowly. Death is so enormous as to be incomprehensible and can be absorbed only over time. As in *Mrs Dalloway*, "death's enormous sickle had swept those tremendous hills …" I feel myself dropped into a gloomy tunnel without markers, without any way to see or feel. And then comes pain so terrible, so searing, it goes beyond colour. It will have no shape and seemingly no end. Eventually, it will shape me. I am worn out by my grieving and yearning for you, Gordon. I am nothing. My grief is bottomless.

54

This Is What I've Made of My Life

I've learned from various sources that in your early years you, Gordon, had a difficult relationship with your father. He didn't, or couldn't, relate to your love of learning, your absorbing of information, nor realize the extent of your mathematical genius that eventually led you to computer science. Your father thought you needed to be toughened up, more like your younger brother, Murray, outdoors playing sports. It was you who told me about the time you phoned your dad.

"Hi, Dad, this is your number one son."

"Hello, Murray," your father said.

Ouch!

Eventually, much of this changed when, finally, your father began to comprehend your singular achievements.

I think about this when again on our bed summoning images of you, a vision comes to me of your parents standing in the doorway of their northern home in Cobalt. They're searching an empty horizon, and I wonder if it's for a glimpse of you approaching. Shading their eyes, they lift them over acres of mown grass, over trees that line the Montreal River, over the gravelled road that runs up to the house. They catch sight of you trekking up that road toward them. In your arms, you're holding your life. You stand before them. You lay it at their feet. Looking up at them, smiling, you say, "Mom, Dad, this is what I've made of my life." A humble smile appears, that shy expression in your eyes, a diffidence from an earlier time.

Love and joy leap into your mother's face when she sees all that you are, all you've become. Your father, his eyes so often like a desert storm, or rock-hard, or with the chill of a wintry night in them, now light up like a summer sky. He stretches out his hands to you, inclines his head. Knowledge of your accomplishments wipe out all the early years of unfounded judgments, the disappointments. Awe and immense pride fill the space.

I want to visit your father, this Murray Watts Senior, in the afterlife to tell him about you, this first-born son who, to the world who knew you, was the true measure of a fine and great man: brilliant, humble, wise, and kind with a heart as generous as that of a saint. To tell him you saw the best in everyone and that "You weren't inclined to criticize," as a colleague said of you. In your professional life, you became not only a mining engineer but a mineral economist, a theoretical mathematician, a pioneer of computer systems.

But again, who were you, Gordon Watts? I seem always to be looking for you.

You formed your own corporation and called it Log II Systems Inc., specializing in computer applications for the mining industry. An early expert in the economic analysis of new mining projects, you employed computer modelling. At the same time, you developed the Log II core logging program, which integrated field exploration data into a computer database to provide high-quality field reports and graphical presentations. You successfully sold this system to a variety of major companies and universities around the world.

This means that you became a pioneer in computer data processing for mineral projects, all DOS-based, simple to use, that, in effect, provided a breakthrough in efficient data transmission and processing, especially for exploration projects. Those data systems and software programs were purchased by the Canadian federal government and the European Commission, and as I mentioned, were sold around the world. You continued this work right into your seventies.

One of your main clients was Watts, Griffis and McEwan (WGM). You were an associate there for more than forty years. For them, you provided economic analysis for teams carrying out due-diligence investigations, for studying the feasibility of a wide variety of projects that were key valuations for the company. This work took you to many countries: Yemen, Myanmar, Saudi Arabia, and Peru. You were involved in a tax interpretation and royalty case in Greece, and on an arbitration panel in Singapore. Your expertise was required on other arbitration panels to interpret mining taxation, leading to a number of expert witness assignments, including one for the European Commission as well as in countries as diverse as Greece and Singapore. Really! Not least, you travelled to remote parts of our own country.

You became a trusted adviser to many mining executives and managers, and I know you were quietly proud of the contributions you made to the successful development of many mining projects. In later years, you were a director of Baffinland Iron, Cuervo Resources, and Mandalay Resources.

It's quite a legacy you left the mining industry.

"Gordon was essentially a theoretical mathematician," brother Murray tells me, and I see now how you loved to weigh things, to measure them.

You created financial models and charts for our everyday purchases, assigning each a code that eventually told us what was spent in various categories. Sometimes your voice drifted down the stairs to tell me that we didn't spend much on entertaining that month but that groceries were up. "Your fault," I'd say delightedly. "It's because you keep inviting all these people to dinner."

"What exactly is a mineral economist?" Matt asks at your funeral, and proceeds to give a dictionary definition. "It is the academic discipline that investigates and promotes understanding of economic and policy issues associated with the production and use of mineral commodities."

I was, and am, in awe of your intelligence, your knowledge and expertise about subjects I know nothing about, and it's to my lasting shame I could never even find the questions to ask.

You, this quiet man in your Distillery District condo in your life before me typically read news from around the world, worked at your desk. Around noon, you strolled over to the English bakery inside the gates of the Distillery to purchase a roast beef sandwich, one-half for lunch, the other for dinner. In the afternoons, a workout on your exercise bike, showering, dressing, then more work, sometimes reading for the remainder of the afternoon and early evening. Occasionally, you wandered the city, met a colleague downtown, a friend at the St. Lawrence Market on Saturdays. Sunday evenings you dined with your sister, Mary.

55

A Prankster

I'm still looking for more of you, Gordon, wanting to know about your university years. I'm particularly intrigued when your friend, Lee Barker, calls you a prankster. Neither Lee, nor any of your colleagues, knows to this day whether you were the one to instigate the kidnapping of a civil engineering fellow one free weekend. The poor fellow was eventually traded back in exchange for some beer.

On another occasion, and again no one has ever figured out whether you were involved on a particular night in a survey camp when all the air was let out of the tires of a professor who was partying with your teachers at the camp.

Lee, accused of being the perpetrator, was ordered out of bed, given a bicycle pump, and told to start pumping at one in the morning.

"Gord shows up," Lee tells me.

"What are you doing?" Gordon asked him.

"What does it look like? I'm half asleep and getting blisters on my hands."

"Gord just grinned at me and went back to bed," Lee tells me.

There were other incidents where it was suspected Gordon was involved in pranks during his university life.

What an interesting bunch of colleagues you had — ones who remain friends to this day.

56

What We Owe the Dead Once More

What do we owe the dead? I've asked. How can I be faithful to you in your death? To remember your birthday, your death day? Wear your clothes, read the books you read? Prepare the food you enjoyed?

I'm wearing some of your T-shirts, your socks. I plan to have some of your summer shirts resized to fit me. This way, and in every way, you'll live with me forever in my heart, my bones, my brain, even when I'm surrounded by others, even when I'm engaged with activities you can no longer personally share with me. I'll take you to bed with me each night and hope to dream of you, and during the day, have you hovering somewhere close to me.

I'm still looking for you, Gordon. Perhaps it's weird to go searching for you after you're gone from the earth. I should use the word *died*, which usually I do. Most people say "passed away." But you died. I've mentioned that Matt joins me in wanting to get to know you better. For both of us, this is ironic. It's sad. Perhaps you love most what you don't quite understand, that you still look for what you feel has been taken from you, or perhaps not given to you. Or is it that the further you're removed from a person you've loved and lost, the more positive, the more sublime they seem?

What would you say of yourself, Gordon? That you left a legacy, made life easier and better for your colleagues? Yes!

Perhaps you might add that you wish you revealed more of yourself to Matt to make his life easier.

Faithfully, I read some of your *Scientific American* and mining magazines. I try to read your books about the cosmos, about the Big Bang …

"What of your son, Matt?" I ask suddenly, and one day after you're gone, Matt and I have a discussion about the differences between the two of you. You weigh and measure. He creates. He's the playwright, the stand-up comic, the actor, the storyteller. Then I find a high school essay you wrote, and the question is: "What is meant by tragedy in Shakespeare using one particular play to illustrate."

You chose *King Lear* and earned an A. I read that essay and understand — perhaps for the first time — what exactly is meant by a Shakespearean tragedy. So, though you were primarily analytical, you had some creativity, too.

Then I recall that on a cold, wintry night you got up and accompanied Dvora Levinson and me to Tarragon Theatre. Enthusiasm was in your posture, and I wondered at you, the engineer, the scientist, jumping up to see an Anton Chekhov play, partly to be read aloud, partly acted. Squeezed into a third-floor attic room, we watched three players under bare light bulbs on a bare stage. One quipped that management reluctantly agreed to turn on the lights. You sit deeply engrossed to the end, and such was your pleasure that you signed a book expressing your interest in further such plays.

Again, why?

Curiosity. And to be with me, to share my interests as in the case of the afternoons of Turkish studies, to share my endless fascination with Turkey and its history and people. You made it all yours — ours.

• • •

Tonight, I'm at a meditation group at the little Anglican church on Dundas Street. I'm supposed to be meditating, though my thoughts are of you, but when are they not? In my mind, I'm in my condo in the Distillery, waiting to leave for the last time, to leave my home and T., though he already left me long ago. All my last-minute stuff is packed, and I'm staying until the buyers come because I've promised them a quick visit before they take possession.

I see my future with you, Gordon, as a shimmering physical reality and am sparked with immeasurable joy. Beyond the windows, clouds take shape, the sky turns pink and stretches to infinity. In my next vision, I see you walking many parts of the earth and in remote places, always with a soft footfall. The world might look to see you walking so beautifully across the earth.

57

Early Images

Without obstacles can there be passion? This query is posed in Gabriel García Márquez's novel *Love in the Time of Cholera*. When we're in love, what is it we're longing for? What do we feel we lack? Do we turn ourselves in the direction we want to look? And do we have to encounter ourselves in another before we recognize ourselves?

I don't have answers to those questions, only that if all else remained in the world and you did not, the world would become to me a dull and lifeless thing, as it has! In fact, I often don't want to be any part of it. I take myself back to the time when I first met and came to know you, and the remembering brings an immensity that wraps itself around me in a golden haze that's cloudless, weightless. Perhaps I dwell too much in my memories, but they also come to me unbidden.

Early in our acquaintance, I invite you to dinner and add, "Please feel free to invite a friend."

"No one comes to mind," you say.

I repeat this when inviting you to a New Year's Eve party.

Again, you answer, "No one comes to mind."

Images of you at that party come to me now, how beautiful you look in your dark blue suit and with the tie that has unicorns on it — my favourite. How tall you stand, how elegant, how perfect you are, and were. If, as Charlotte Brontë says in *Jane Eyre* in the voice of one of her characters about another character, that "he was of the material from which Nature hews her heroes ... her statesmen, her conquerors," then I declare you to have been such a man but moulded differently. You were a self-contained, self-propelled, quiet hero with a big presence.

You were a castle, and I love castles!

Am I to be condemned to weeping over my vivid images of you, searching for you and for all the remembrances of what we did and how we were? Or do I live, knowing that all these feelings, these recollections, will eventually fade? Will they, and should they?

Today, I'm upstairs in your office to do a thirty-minute workout on the elliptical machine. There are your pajamas, shorts, running shoes, sweatbands still exactly where you left them. I stare at them, as I always do, and today, feel the life in them has dimmed, your spirit infusing them has paled, and I'm deeply sad, worried even, that you might fade from me, even though I can't imagine that happening. Every night before I go to bed, I look compulsively at photos of you, a habit that both comforts and saddens me.

All those times when in my mind I go looking for you, so often I return to those years when you travelled to Australia to work for six months, then roamed Southeast Asia. From tales I've heard, you moved to your own internal command. I have visions of you in and out of the homes of local people in Singapore, Thailand, Japan, Indonesia, Taiwan, Norway. From these places, you bring prints and bolts of cloth, which I have and treasure. You bring statues of the Buddha in various poses, carpets from Persia, soapstone carvings from the Arctic. You make friends, learn about the world, offer assistance. You work for room and board.

Other contrasting images take shape: you in the mines of Ontario's North, in the mountains of Peru, in remote Uzbekistan. I see you in the Baffin Land Iron Ore mines, but apparently you never did work inside a mine.

What brought you home?

"If you keep travelling, you won't be able to stop." That's what you've been told. As well, you hear that many of your friends and some of your siblings are marrying and beginning to have children. Time to go home. Time to look for a partner, a wife, have children. Then there's your beloved mother waiting for you.

You return to Canada to work at WGM. You meet Mureille, an elegant young woman working in a secretarial capacity at the company. You marry her.

58

A Professional Life

One day, I'm in the basement hunting for junk to discard. I find your Arctic coat and can scarcely pick it up, judging it to weigh about a hundred pounds.

"Guaranteed to keep you warm up to minus sixty degrees," you once told me. Minus sixty degrees — yikes!

"Is that when you were working in B.C. near the border with Alaska?" I asked then.

And in my mind, we're in the basement together, you putting up shelves, me sorting all the paraphernalia we've collected. You pick up your coat, wrap me up in it, and I disappear inside it. I recall this, remembering the tales of your northern adventures when, suddenly, I'm in a treeless, featureless Arctic winter with you, heading for Watts Lake. Yes, your father named a lake after the family, another after his daughter, Mary, yet another after second son, Murray, and a river after you — Gordon River. Again, I see you in that Arctic coat, ice crystals clinging to your eyelashes, strands of hair escaping your woollen hat, pinpoints of blue behind sunglasses.

I've returned to the basement to sort your stuff, alone now since your spirit seems to have gone somewhere. I find rollerblades, more outerwear, leggings, other heavy jackets, also your skates and clothing for skating, including helmets, goggles, gloves — and you the man, the boy, your father forced outdoors and insisted on your being toughened up!

Tired now, beginning again to weep for you, so emotional — but when am I not? — I drop into a chair, conjuring you in that rugged, lonely Arctic clime, imagining a life in and around mining sites dominated by shrill whistles signalling shift changes, the constant roar of rock crushers and an acrid smell of toxic mine tailings. I see you, a vigorous young man, climbing around rocks and trees and lakes scattered over an otherwise bleak and empty terrain, your curiosity primed about the mineral secrets of an earth hiding its treasures. Did you work to your own timetable up there? And what exactly did you do? I google "field engineer." This it what I get:

> Field engineers are on-site technicians who troubleshoot issues and problems with equipment or systems. They can work in a variety of different sectors depending on the area of engineering they specialize in. This job involves applying theories to address problems, writing reports to outline these issues and solutions, and working with companies to help develop more efficient systems. This job is well suited to analytical and critical thinkers

who can apply logic and theories to problems, have the patience to find resolutions to complex issues, and have strong communication skills.

Much of this, if not all of it, suits you very well. I include this to give a flavour of the work you did:

> On November 25, 2010, the parliament of Mongolia adopted an amendment to Article 47. The amendment introduced a new surtax royalty that was applicable from January 1, 2011. The amendment does not modify the standard royalty regime.
>
> A surtax royalty is imposed on the total sales value of 23 types of minerals in addition to the standard flat-rate royalty previously applicable.
>
> The new surtax royalty replaces a previously applicable windfall profits tax.
>
> The rates of the surtax royalty vary depending on the type of minerals, their market prices, and their degree of processing.
>
> More specifically, the rates are significantly higher for copper than for other types of minerals; the rates increase as the market prices for the minerals go up; and the rates are lower for processed materials than for unprocessed minerals in order to encourage mining companies to engage in value-added activities.
>
> For copper, the surtax royalty rates range between 22% and 30% for ore, between 11% and 15% for concentrates, and between 1% and 5% for final products. Reference prices with their sources are announced from government organizations on a quarterly basis.

Well, then! For me, it's like trying to decipher a foreign language without ever having seen it written or heard spoken. But I try. I struggle to comprehend a bunch of theoretical physicists discussing a universe where space and time aren't fundamental; where new physics theories posit that these aren't real; where there may be a deeper, abstract mathematical reality to the universe than what we perceive ...

And so I struggle on.

59
Young and Old Life

How difficult it is for you to adjust to the rigidity of life as you perceive your friends and colleagues living it, to attune yourself to the usual timetable where most people go to work at nine in the morning and come home at five — the rat race? Is that a term recently invented? You dislike expectations that aren't yours, dislike the bellicose orders and dictates of your father.

Your travelling has to end sometime, of course, and you return to what you know, to your family, and adjust to life in North America. Not least, to working for your father and becoming an employee of WGM.

Ultimately, you resign. I'm not sure of the circumstances, but perhaps because you refuse to do what's being imposed and you're angry with your father. Then you're on your way to the farthest corner of northwestern British Columbia bordering Alaska, the place where you wore that Arctic coat. You drive across an endless landscape in wintry conditions, arriving amid a snowstorm in a Morris Minor that has but a tiny pinpoint on your windscreen through which to see. You emerge a solid white mass, frozen to your very marrow.

Once more in Toronto, you work at WGM. Among your titles you're an entrepreneur, an associate, and a consultant. Eventually, you open an office at 80 Front Street with your own company, Log II Systems Inc. You're at Market Square where you live with your wife and son. At first you're successful but struggle to maintain your business during economic downturns, eventually losing it in the early 1990s.

Whenever we drive around Toronto, you point out the places where you lived over the course of twelve, thirteen years, most of them alone. All were small one-room flats here and there all over the city. Laughingly, I call you a nomad. Now you can say you live in comparative luxury in this Victorian house of ours.

Your sister, Mary, enters that house after we decorate it, after we bought paintings, new furniture, and some sculptures, after we laid new floors, painted walls that gleam in soft yellows, deep blues, and burnished browns. She stands in the living room, looks around her, and says, as she has before, "You know, to think that Gordon was such an awkward, shy, and solitary man always drifting from one small apartment to another. He never really had a home. Now he's got you. He's got all this!"

60

Afterward

I'm back walking those corridors in my mind, the long stretches in our condo at the Distillery, also the long hall in our Berkeley Street house. (I walked along it one day recently and intense grief hit me because the carpet laid upon it is the very one we carried back from Cappadocia in Turkey.) I wander through our uninhabited rooms where your shape sometimes appears. Where you come most often to me is in our bedroom near white cupboard doors where your shirts and socks are. In the walk-in closet. In the bathroom after a shower. Your silhouette is in the doorway, then you're opening the closets to find your T-shirts and socks. Now you're striding out of the bathroom we argued over, I lamenting the mess of it with your stuff piled haphazardly all over its counters. Now I cry when I recall the words between us, and like a child promising its mother, I tell you that I'll keep my stuff off it, won't mess it up, and it's okay for you to have your things piled everywhere.

I can never keep that promise to you.

There's nothing I can fix.

My huge heartache never leaves me because your past and present selves keep materializing, and if they don't, I summon them. All your clothes are still in the walk-in closet with mine, some of your shirts stitched from the faintest blue sky, others from woodland violets, the blue of a robin's egg. You loved that colour, and it suited perfectly the summer blue of your eyes. What shall I do with your clothes? I can't imagine a day when I'll ever want to move them. Then I think of souls: perhaps they live on in perpetual echoes, in silhouettes in doorways, roaming long corridors? I don't know ...

My regrets continue to come out of the never-ending cold and rainy days of that first year, one that isn't finished yet as I write this. I think of all the little things I could or should have done better, and putting them together makes for endless evenings of regrets and tears.

"But think of what you had," my granddaughter tells me. "Think about the long time span and not individual moments of your time together." Such wisdom from one so young!

"You changed after meeting me" — that's what many people say, and it makes me smile.

Something else I love about you, sweetie, is how you always refer to me when with other people by my name. You say, "Carolyn has already heard this, but ..." So many refer to their spouses in front of them as she/he/her/him. Then, when pouring wine for guests, first you offer me a glass. Such love and respect you show me. Thank you.

I think again about how you love to weigh and measure things, and in our kitchen are measuring cups, but you don't do the cooking! Utensils, funnels for your flax seed appear, and scales, too, but I'm not sure what those are for, and I smile at the idea of your baking. Upstairs in your office, you have eye charts taped to a wall, doctor's office weigh scales, measuring tapes.

And I: the opposite end of the — guess what? — scale. Typically, I guess the amounts I need when I bake. I make do. I improvise. You're methodical, careful, analytical, while I fly by the seat of my pants, always in a hurry in everything I do.

How ever did we manage? Perfectly in harmony — that's how!

61

Shadows Creeping

That last long weekend in May our family plans to drive to Kingston to visit granddaughter Cameron and her newly rented house — she's a second-year student at Queen's University — to see what she needs to furnish it. Expectations are high that we'll enjoy ourselves in this historic, pretty little place on the St. Lawrence River. What's not to look forward to?

It's Saturday, May 18, and a cold but clear, sunny day when we set off. You drive the whole distance, Gordon, which surprises me because more often than not you say the light isn't good for you to see well enough to take the wheel.

Each family rents rooms in the same hotel in downtown Kingston, finds a place to have lunch, then goes out to see the rented house.

Afterward, you, Jim, Cameron, and Rachel walk it, while Graeme and I drive with Helen. Graeme comments in wonder about your ability to walk so far and so long, not knowing how fit you are, not understanding about you and walking, and I see images of you striding open roads with wide horizons, on city streets with their noises, lights, hustle, and among the occasional freak shows around where we live. We stroll the waterfront, gather in groups, and chat.

Saturday evening we're all in an Italian restaurant, together with Cameron's friend, Robert. I sit down toward the end of the table where the young ones are and enjoy a lively conversation about many things, including comparing the way in which the Canadian and American governments treat Indigenous people.

I wonder afterward whether you were quiet, Gordon, but can't really say one way or another.

Sunday morning is again cold but sunny. We join Graeme for breakfast in the hotel, then you and I search the shops selling kettles and such things we think Cameron needs. We meet up, find a restaurant for lunch, then after, amble about the open market looking at paintings, books, and other objects.

Gathered one last time at the waterfront, Jim takes a group photo. My understanding is that Jim will drive home with us, but he doesn't, and you and I head off on our own, you slipping into the driver's seat. I feel a keen letdown for unknown reasons other than that the weekend so anticipated is now over and we're going home alone.

I set about to cheer us up — myself, anyway — and launch into what I hope will be a discussion about Indigenous people and where they stand in today's world and in Ontario. It's normally a subject you're interested in, but I can't engage you, and you remain almost stubbornly quiet the entire three-and-a-half-hour drive home.

That evening, as we sit in front of the television, I raise a question about my new novel, but as on the drive home, you don't connect with me. Throughout the evening, you remain largely silent. I interpret that you're bored with the subject of my novel and let it drop. Now I wonder if the wings of death were hovering, brushing up close to you.

Afterward, I can't recall what we did on the holiday Monday, though I rack my mind searching. And in the never-ending days after, when I'm with Susan Dineen, I tell her I can't remember that day.

"Oh, I do," she says. "Terry and I had coffee with you in your house that afternoon."

"Really! Where's my memory? What did we talk about?"

"Oh, lots of things, including the high cost of funerals."

Ouch! But still my mind continues to remain a blank about that last day.

62

Shadows Gathering

Sometime during those last two days your face draws away into shadows. I can't engage you much in conversation, as on the way home from Kingston, even with a subject you've always been interested in. You speak little and seem not prepared to share your thoughts. But then sometimes you don't.

Whatever we watch on television that night I don't remember, or the time we go to bed. Neither of us is to know that we're living the last hours of our lives together, that this is the final night we'll be in bed together.

On Tuesday, May 21, we have breakfast together in the sunroom as always — well, except for those times when one of us brings the other breakfast in bed. I go upstairs to get ready for an appointment at Mount Sinai Hospital, leaving about 9:15 a.m. "Bye, sweetie," I call as I go out the door.

I get intravenous infusions of a biological drug every eight weeks for treatment of rheumatoid arthritis. It takes up the morning. I read while I'm there, go to the lab for blood tests afterward, and then begin the long walk home along Gerrard Street to Berkeley. I can't recall my thoughts as I walk, most likely on one of my short stories then in progress, perhaps dwelling on the difficulties getting my last novel published.

Some people believe there's a premonition of lurking disaster, of life's end. I do not. The wings of death don't brush against me; no cold draft of it comes anywhere close.

I reach the front door to find it unlocked. *Oh!* Usually, you check it on your way upstairs. A tiny ripple of surprise runs through me. I call out, get no answer, but that's not uncommon because often you don't hear me when you're on the third floor. I walk the long corridor into the kitchen — a corridor of restlessness as in the poem that will later speak to me. I make a cup of coffee and carry it up to my office on the second floor, then call out again. Still no answer. Well, you might be in the shower, so wouldn't hear me. No, you're not there. A little puzzled now, I look in the back bedroom, then begin climbing the stairs to the third floor and your office.

I'm almost at the top when I see you.

"Gordon?"

In your desk chair, you're a little slumped forward, your head resting on your chest. Immediately, I notice blood dried on your face, some vomit on your shirt. I see at once — or do I? Gasping, I rush to you.

"Gordon? Gordon!"

I feel for your pulse — none. I put my hand under your nose to feel for air — *no, no, no!* "But you must just be unconscious!" I yell, and run for my phone to dial 911. Sheer terror momentarily zaps me, and the beginning of the creeping horror to come, but at this moment I'm numb. I think nothing. I feel nothing …

A voice says, "Get him out of the chair and onto the floor. Start chest compressions."

I grab your feet and try to pull you out of the chair, but you're literally deadweight, all six feet of you and about one hundred and eighty pounds. Crying now, I race down the two flights of stairs and outside.

"Can anyone help me? Help me!"

Vanessa Tanner from two doors up is in her front garden and dashes over. Together, we hurry up the stairs, but before we can try again to remove you from the chair, the medics come.

Immediately, they set themselves the task of restarting your heart, which eventually they do. But my foreboding is complete. I know your heart is vigorous, but you'll have suffered irreparable brain damage from loss of oxygen, regardless of the cause of your death. I jump in the ambulance to go to St. Michael's Hospital with you, sit beside you holding your hand, whisper to you. Various medical specialists come in and out of your emergency room, and while you're being investigated, I sit alone in a chair in an unlit corridor. Staff members come to ask if I need help, shouldn't I have someone with me?

I'm in a fog, in shock. I'm there, but not there — not anywhere. I shake my head as though to alter my reality.

The enormity of your death can't be digested. It's much too large to be processed, and it will be a long time before I really grasp what's happened. It's said that dying people might appear unconscious, and that when all other organs fail, often they retain their hearing, so I sit beside you holding your hand, whispering, "I love you, I love you, don't go. Don't go!" All the while your heart beats heroically. But even as I talk to you, tell you as I've told you those too-few years we were married, *I just love you so much*, I know you're not there, know you're already gone.

I realize that family members, especially your son, Matt, have a right to know what's happened, so eventually I get up, but not having my phone with me, begin walking out of the hospital, out onto Shuter Street, and then the twenty-minute trek home.

I feel old.

I feel nothing.

Late-afternoon shadows fall across the pavement. Young people play ball in Moss Park. Traffic courses the city streets. The light is grey, flat, the world dull, colourless. I'm everywhere and nowhere. I can't think, can't feel, only that I'm moving mechanically in a tunnel that feels like an absence of everything — a giant sucking void.

I go straight into Rick's house next door. He's been home and has heard nothing. Greg comes over. We sit in the sunroom and talk about you, Gordon, the particular and fine man they both feel you to be, and immediately it comforts me. Together, we return to the hospital. Both men make phone calls to inform the family.

We gather in a hospital emergency room where you lie on a bed covered lightly with a sheet up to your neck, all six feet of you, appearing as though you're just sleeping and now with good colour since you're being oxygenated.

You look big and beautiful.

You are dead.

We all stand around the bed looking at the terrible beauty of you. You appear alive and tranquil, as if you're just resting. As I gaze at you, images come to me: your long-limbed, unhurried stride; your constant, quiet, measured demeanour amid the cacophony of the world.

The neurologist approaches me. "Your husband has had a massive brain hemorrhage," he says. "I'm afraid his brain is dead. We're keeping him on life support but will need to make a decision when to remove it. If you want to be absolutely sure, we can scan his brain."

They do. The scan shows massive, irretrievable brain death.

You're dead. I feel dead.

The family arrives. Suzanne happens to be in Toronto from Oregon. Mary, David, Jean-Yves, Paloma, Anik, Matt, Helen, Jim, Cameron, Rachel, and then Greg and Rick have all come. Perhaps Annika is there, too, and Peter Lepik. Your nephew and nieces talk about you, how they called you Uncle Tree when they were young because you stood with arms stretched wide while your small nephew and nieces climbed all over you. Now we stand around your bed looking at your beautiful form lying there. We weep. I'm not sure I do. I can't assimilate what just happened. But my tears flow uncontrollably and frequently for more than a year as I write this, and during all those never-ending days and weeks when the enormity of what happened finally registers.

That same night, two police officers knock on the door of our house. Apologetically, they say they're required by law to investigate any death that occurs at home. So I trudge with them to the third floor, to your office. "If you want to see the scene of the crime, here it is," I say, hearing the bitterness in my voice.

The following day, I sit in the chair where you died, the chair that will forever remain empty. I shout down the two flights of stairs, "No! No, no, no!"

And then my weeping begins, weeping that hasn't stopped yet. *I love you! Love you! I miss you!*

And so begins the rest of my life … without you.

63

Your Life: *Vita, Gloriosa Vita*

Gordon darling, you should have been at your funeral! It seems to me that the entire world has come to pay homage to you: your large family, your many colleagues, friends of yours from over all the years. And my family, my friends, and those we made in our short life together. Members of my writers' group come, and my two book clubs. Elsewhere, they arrive from Oregon, British Columbia, Calgary, from all over Ontario. Not least, my sister and brother-on-law from New Zealand.

"In lieu of flowers, send donations to the Children's Book Bank on Berkeley Street," I request. Yes, to Berkeley Street. But no nightingales are singing now.

To me, everything is a blur, even while I've arranged it all. I wear black. I feel calm. I'm dead inside, and my expression is as bleak as are my emotions. The crowds are so large they can't be accommodated in the room set up, so are moved to the larger chapel. I stand against a wall as people file past me, glance at me, then away. I see only a stream of empty faces, my thoughts as black as my clothes.

My neighbour, Rick — the Very Reverend Richard Fee — conducts the ceremony. He's our next-door neighbour and friend, the reverend who has conducted all the major events in the life of my extended family.

"There is no one here today," he begins, "who thought that such a gathering was conceivable just one week ago — even one day ago … 'Short days ago, we lived, felt dawn, saw sunset glow, loved and were loved and now we lie …' As for mortals, their days are like grass — they flourish like the flower of the field. The wind passes over it, and it is gone, and its place knows it no more.

"We want Gordon's legacy to be carried forward," Rick says, "because we saw in his life values that have inspired us and we hope those values have now taken root in our own lives."

He speaks of the mystery of being human, that we live our lives knowing nothing is guaranteed. But when death comes, it is unique, deeply personal, like a sudden interruption.

"Humans can imagine the impossible," Rick continues. "Humans sing, dance, compose music. Humans tinker with surroundings … humans have a large brain for thinking and guessing. Humans create and destroy on purpose. Humans write poetry and equations. Humans believe in right versus wrong … humans weep for the loss of a loved one. Humans remember their grandparents and earlier ancestors. Humans laugh."

Then he adds, "Gordon's death has given us pause. It has given us much to ponder. In this intelligent, humble, easygoing 'Uncle Tree,' we saw a man who was a problem-solver, a man who had no ego, who loved his solitary life and was happy in his own company. He shared love, was fulfilled in his relationship with Carolyn, and garnered respect from his colleagues around the world … It is a beautiful world because Gordon was here, and so much remains of what he contributed to make it beautiful. While his physical presence has been removed, his professional accomplishments, his encouraging words, his warm nature, are not forgotten. What remains is the good that he did, the lessons he shared, the time he took to instruct. These are his legacy."

Rick finishes with these words: "We bid farewell to such a soul as we have been privileged to know … that now and forever, the day breaks and the shadows flee away."

No! The day might break, but shadows do not flee away!

I walk to the podium next to tell the assembled crowd about you, my beloved. I say that at our wedding I described you as a beautiful man, and ten years later I'm still telling the world you are a beautiful man. "For those who haven't been lucky enough to know you," I continue, "I'd like to say this — that you were a giant of a man with a brilliant mind, together with a vast knowledge of the world. And yet you were humble, always understated — 'a man without an ego,' an old friend once commented. To me, to anyone who met you, this is, and was, an irresistible combination.

"You found it more interesting to ask questions of others rather than talk about yourself," I say. "Your deep generosity drove you to work quietly behind the scenes on others' behalf, always trying to solve their particular problem — for family, friends, acquaintances, the whole world you knew.

"This solitary man I supposed you to be when first knowing you also embraced and enjoyed company. You would ask me, 'What's on for this week, or this weekend?' If I said not much, you expressed disappointment, and so I cite you as an example of an adaptable man, wise, mature.

"I, or anybody, could discuss anything with you — world affairs, philosophy, politics, you always being right, of course! I, on the other hand, am very social, so off we went to untold numbers of social, cultural, and family events." I want to tell much more but become emotional and stop.

I say to anyone who asks that we were always together. We walked side by side, you at six feet in height and I a mere five foot three. We travelled, attended concerts, book clubs, opera, theatre, and dinner with friends. I mention happiness, as in the Robert Frost poem, the issue for me being that you are flooded with happiness yet don't know that you are, or that you have it — this state of being called happiness. How can you appreciate what you have at the time you have it? Can it only be afterward?

Gordon, I want to tell you that you helped me in everything. You were like a giant: strong and powerful, a bulwark and a backstop to everything I did. In my eulogy to you, I say that with you I felt free to be and do a hundred things, a thousand things, while you did what you've always done: working, physically working out, reading. Ah, reading, and I cite some of it: *The Joy of a Guided Tour of Math from One to Infinity, Fooled by Randomness: The Hidden Role of Chance in Life, The Cosmic Web: The Mysterious Architecture of the Universe.*

A friend says to try not to mourn too much the loss of the flame Gordon cast but to celebrate how brightly it glowed in your life. I would add: "It glows in the lives of all those lucky enough to have known you."

I was, and am, very proud of you! I loved you with all my heart, my soul, and all the bones in my body and would give, oh, so much, to have more time with you. But when I'm able to lament less, I'll be able to cherish more the memories of my unbelievably good fortune to have been with you.

My small writers' group says: "We got to know who Gordon was through your eyes, as well as through the other tributes by his son, sisters, brothers, and one of his best friends. Your next-door neighbour was the consummate MC. We loved the music — an eclectic blend of hymns, classical music, and some rock and roll by The Doors. Gordon certainly led an interesting and fulfilling time on this earth, and from what we could gather, his happiest years were spent with you, Carolyn. We were honoured to be able to bear witness to his life."

In his eulogy for you, your son, Matt, says, "We did love each other, in our way. We never expressed it, or said it, but we knew it was there. Like I know there's a North Pole. I've never been, but I've seen pictures. And compasses point to it! As my father would say, 'There is evidence.' This last chapter of his life with Carolyn was the happiest chapter. He was a different person with her. He smiled a lot more, he laughed a lot more — there was a lightness to him that I'd never seen, and because of that, he was different with me. He was more fun, more caring, and more honest, because, Carolyn, he loved you. He loved you so much. With you, I didn't have to look for evidence. It was there. It was like you were the North Pole. And I know why, I can see why. You are genuinely one of the most wonderful people I've ever met, and my heart breaks for you and my father. You were the best thing in his life, and you deserved so much more time together."

Your sister, Mary, says: "Gordon had a magnificent mind that held millions of historic information. He had knowledge about everything, including all we ever wanted to know about our complex family history. He had a very dry sense of humour and liked to buy his siblings funny gifts. For Robert, an army helmet after he crashed his motorcycle. For Mimi, a bust of Chopin for her to put on the grand piano. For me, a Second World War bulletproof vest to protect my 'assets.'

"He had the patience of a saint in looking after our mother in her great age, teaching her to use the computer after she was eighty and almost blind. Our brother, Gordon, was brainy, courageous, witty, loyal, determined, and stubborn. I'm going to find life difficult without him ... I cannot tell you how much I loved him, and I speak for my brothers and sisters when I say this."

Maria Flannery, a long-time friend who hosted our wedding, tells me, "You had a great understanding and love for one another and it's a pity that it finished so suddenly."

Your colleague and good mate, Lee Barker, says of you: "You always seemed to have a tiny smile on your face like you knew something no one else did, and we all suspected you had a bit of the prankster in you. You were always surprising us. For example, you forgot the Christmas lunch, but being the keeper of our annual forecasts for metal prices, you came late after a phone call."

Your cousin, Barb, tells me, "You two had such a beautiful relationship. You were, in my opinion, a most adorable couple, always with smiles on your faces and giggling like teenagers. How beautiful to have that in your life."

Another friend says, "I loved being around you two."

Much more of this kind has been said to me, and it was all exactly like that. Sometimes, when remembering those eulogies, I marvel that you, this man, seemingly so ordinary, who empties the dishwasher, the cat litter box, shops for groceries, and fixes the garage door, is this same man who quietly accomplishes so much.

And now it's back to our empty house — now my house. That day, and those that come after, I go upstairs and sit in the now-empty chair where you sat, where you died. The shadows that creep about me are only pushed away when I summon the embers of our love story, then relive them.

64

After

The immediate days after ... after ... I can't even breathe the word ... when I awake each morning it's to a renewed horror, my eyes opening to a landscape strewn with ashes.

At times, in those first days after the funeral, I roar around in a frenzy, frantic to clean up, to tidy, to fix. Ah, to fix: it's just come to me that there's nothing I can do to fix this and bring you back, so I clean, fix physical things in the house. Those scuff marks on the baseboards in the dining room — paint them. I do. Next, the scratch marks on the powder room door — gone. About to start painting the basement door, I stop suddenly, my hand holding the paintbrush poised in the air.

"Whatever are you doing?" I stare at myself. "You don't have to do this!" Tired, perspiring, I put down the brush, sit on the top basement step, and peer into the darkness below, consumed and overcome by sadness. "You really don't have to do this. It's not important," I repeat aloud, and so talking to myself, I quit my cleanup and fix-up activities.

I think the brute truth that you're dead only fully hits me when I, together with David's son, Jean-Yves, attend a service at St. Michael's Hospital for those whose loved ones have recently died there, and though you actually died at home, technically it was at that hospital. About a dozen of us are ushered into a room set up as a chapel, and as we enter, flowers are placed in our hands, mine a gerbera. After a short service accompanied by sacred music, each of us is invited to stand, place our flowers in a vase on a table, and announce the name of our deceased loved one.

It dawns on me when my turn comes and I get up that I'm telling myself, telling the world, that you're dead. *Dead.* I absorb it as though for the first time, the nightmarish reality hitting so hard I can scarcely stand. With my head bowed, I try to say the words "my husband, Gordon Watts," but my voice, my tears choke me, and in this extremity of my grief I creep away to find somewhere to hide.

65

Is There Any Life After ...?

The days and weeks tick by. I pick up books and put them down. But I keep trying, since reading was always my joy, my education, my escape, my entertainment. I turn to a book by a Ukrainian novelist recommended to me, with the unlikely title *Field Studies in Ukrainian Sex*. As I read through it, a paragraph jumps out:

> I met a sapling at a crossroads, trembling and rustling. Someone invisible setting a bonfire below, the strike of a match, and in a flash — the sapling is consumed by fire which goes out as soon as it starts, as if it only meant to strip its crown of leaves, and so in the place where a moment earlier the sapling glittered with shades of light green against the blue sky, there now protrudes a bitter, blackened skeleton.

What a metaphor for your untimely and very sudden death. And I left behind!

My sister and brother-in-law from Auckland remain with me for four weeks. People come and go. My daughter hovers, comforting — well, trying to comfort me — as well as my son, my daughter-in-law, my grandchildren, members of the Watts family, and friends near and distant. Neighbours also.

Each morning yawns before me, iron-grey and dull, no features to it. Immediately, I search for snapshots of you and photograph them with my phone. Compulsively, I gaze at them every night in bed. I've had many printed and have propped them all around the kitchen and dining room, but they're not always comforting. Sometimes, on catching sight of you, I'm devastated at my loss all over again.

Days, weeks, pass in a blur. For untold hours, I lie on our bed and summon images of our early life, especially how we set up this house on Berkeley Street. Eventually, I fall asleep fitfully, only to awaken often throughout the night, each time to be hit with a sense of desolation. I see us only yesterday, the young couple we were — well, young in our sixties — on the cusp of an infinite life that shimmers and is the true beginning to our lives. It comes to me again: the sense of you, of us, and of our life before us, of all the ways to infinity.

We are. We do. We were. We remodel the interior of our house on Berkeley Street, as I've mentioned. We purchase paintings together. Not finished yet, we buy new creamy-white leather chairs and couches. We lay rugs, too — fabulous Persian and Turkish ones you bring with you — and woollen ones I have. I tame the garden and plant perennials and annuals, a small bush here and there. It's bliss, it's a beginning that has no end — not that we can see, anyway.

Now, on that matrimonial bed, I see myself alone among all that we built. But by superimposing the past on the present and merging them, for a time I manage to dull my grief. I summon images of you: in a uniform of jeans that you wear all summer right up to the time when July heat soars and humidity thickens around us. Until one day you appear in the corridor outside your condo in beige shorts — awful shorts! — baggy to your knees and full of bulging pockets. But I don't care how you look. And it occurs to me how differently love comes to one. Some, as Elizabeth Alexander says in her memoir *The Light of the World*, "It's love at first sight." For Lorna Crozier in her memoir *Through the Garden*, it's "a fiery collision." For me, it's like a gentle sun that shines brighter and brighter as days and weeks pass, to reach its zenith in a sustained, brilliant glow.

Another memory comes to me, and I tell it here because it shows you in your complexity that's not easily categorized. It's the evening when I return from the writers' group at the Parliament Street Library and rush to you in your condo. You've left your front door open for me, expecting me. You're seated at your computer upstairs, deeply engrossed and seemingly not willing to be interrupted, not even by your new great love. I stand at your side for some moments — or were they minutes? — before you turn around. But when you do, those deep-set eyes focus on me, becoming a soft liquid blue. Never mind those moments when you sit glued to your laptop, I think I understand you and hold a larger view.

And your condo — how chaotic. Upstairs you have an exercise bike with a hook on the back of it where you hang all your clothes, or so it seems. On the floor are discarded papers and hundreds of business cards scattered all over. Curls of dust. Books stacked on the floor. But my abiding image is of you in your kitchen in a chair before your red art deco kitchen table under streaming morning sunlight, newspapers scattered on both the table and floor. I come to learn how much you prize those morning hours with coffee, toast, and newspapers. I'm sure I've said this, but your great pleasure is absorbing knowledge. I also realize you have little need to share that knowledge, only later with me and with others whose company you come to know and enjoy.

Ironically, long will be the days, months, a year, and more when I'll search for further knowledge of you. As I do, images and fragments of conversations come to me, both Mary and David saying you're the go-to person for everything. Someone else says you're an exceptionally kind person, accepting, non-judging. Your colleague, Bob Kuehnbaum, says of you, "Gord wasn't inclined to criticize. He was enduringly cheerful and upbeat, often amused by events and circumstances. And it's hard to forget his laugh."

I love all this!

Gordon, you changed me. No longer do I restlessly rush through the present to get to the next day. No longer does my restless self search for more and yet more mental and emotional stimulation. Because

I've learned that everything that's exhilarating is right in front of me, beside me, and with me.

You were super-brilliant, of course. Why "of course"? Because anyone could see it. Again, as Bob Kuehnbaum tells me, "Gordon's financial systems were nothing short of brilliant, and his prodigious talent for financial modelling was apparent to me right from the start. One day, the two of us are attending a meeting of a dozen or so very senior geoscientists and engineers where a prospective client asks us about our backgrounds. Gord's list runs on from his mining days to operating his own mining software firm. Then being a founder of two mining companies, each of which proved to have enormous resources of iron. Gord was highly accomplished in his profession."

Really! I know I'm building you up to near-mythical, near-saintly proportions when I write all this, but that was how I felt about you all the time we were together. I saw the beautiful bulk of you, your strong limbs moving, how straight you stood. I remember how I rushed to the front-room windows to watch you stride up the street. Walking: again I swear that the entire world looked up at you as you walked so quiet, so beautiful, across the earth.

66

This Is, and Was, Us: Our *Vita, Gloriosa Vita*

Eventually, I begin to go out to dinner with friends here and there, but with tears in my eyes. I come home alone to my door — *I will meet you at the empty door* — to the vacant halls.

"Where are you?" I cry out again. Then: "No. No, no, no!" My voice echoes down the two flights of stairs. "How could you have left me? How *could* you?"

I walk the corridor from the front door to the back — *the corridor of restlessness*. But there's no rest for me. I pick up one photo of you, another and another: you're beside me, looking out at me. One by one,

I kiss them and go up to bed to weep myself to sleep. I've done this most nights since you died.

One day, I pace the hallway downstairs over your Persian rug on the dining room floor. Another day, open the door to the walk-in closet to put clothes into the laundry basket. Yet another, drive into the garage. In each instance, the feeling of aloneness hits me like a blow. It happens at unexpected times and in strange places, also when I do ordinary things.

I purchase Joan Didion's *The Year of Magical Thinking* about her grief after the death of her husband, brood over it, feel tears come in buckets, tears that are always threatening. There I find no consolation, only momentary distraction. My first foray to the Loblaws supermarket, and there's a hard pain over my heart — a contraction or expansion of the magnetic field around it — I'm not sure which.

How does one endure the meaningless of death, the unending absence that follows, the cruel sense of aloneness as one walks down a familiar, or unfamiliar, street? As one drives into a garage, enters a shop, comes home alone?

Another week passes, another month, and I write to you every night to tell you what I do — my one consolation. I miss you fiercely. I feel very much alone, especially when returning home and entering the front or back door from the garage, there you always were, waiting for me. It's lovely, lovely, lovely, the thought and idea of you, to talk to you, be with you and to love you. I roam the streets looking for you. As I've mentioned, anyone coming toward me with a vague resemblance to you causes my heart to stop. It never can be you, and I'm diminished all over again. I long to see you gaze at me just one more time, one last time.

Today, Saturday, I'm doing all the things we both usually do, but doing them alone. I feel like a half-person, a faint shadow. I've been cut in two and idly wonder if I'll ever be stitched together again. Every part of the house has you in it, and the sense of abandonment never leaves me.

Then one day, suddenly, I decide to do some writing. After an hour at my desk editing my "A Man Called George" story, I'm about to call up the stairs to you, "Are you hungry? Are you ready for lunch?"

Silence from up there. Okay. I go downstairs. But you're not in your chair in front of the TV watching Wimbledon, taking in the news, a science documentary. You're not anywhere, and again I think I can't bear it.

Tonight, I'm going out for dinner with friends, but tears lurk. At home again, I call out to the vacant doorways, the empty doors, the chair upstairs where you died. "Where are you?" I hear my voice echo down the two flights of stairs. "How could you have left me? How *could* you?"

In late June, or maybe it's July, I'm invited to your miners' University of Toronto class of 1966 annual luncheon in the Distillery District. Ah, yes, the Distillery and our previous home. While there, I stare up at our old condo building, your condo at one end, mine at the other. Bittersweet memories course through me that I'd met you there, only to lose you, and now you're nowhere.

I enjoy the luncheon until I watch as two by two the couples leave, and it's then I experience the feeling that I'm an *I* when the rest of the world seems to be a *We*.

My son, Paul, flies back east to help me and his dad with technology and other household issues. As he goes through details of practical and technical things with me, I think, *What a mistake to have a division of labour within a household where each does what one knows.* Now I have to learn to do all those things you did, Gordon, that I couldn't do, didn't want to learn. But how wonderful to have my son!

During the week, Paul and I are invited to a barbecue. The old crowd assembles. A lovely summer's day, great food. At one point, the women gather under an awning and the conversation becomes where everyone is headed for vacation. I sit there mute and increasingly depressed. I can't foresee travelling anywhere in any future, and even if I can, it will have to be alone. One thing I do know is that I can't see myself returning to any of those places I spent time with you, Gordon, and this rules out many parts of the world.

Paul returns to the West Coast, and I'm home doing the usual chores: cleaning, gardening, cooking. One night, I dream I'm a stick in a desert, only suddenly to be caught up in the blast of a wintry night. There I stand, battered by winds and rain and snow squalls, trying to figure out who I am. And sometimes in my fierce, relentless agony, I feel more honest, with no face, no voice, no act to assume for anyone. I'm me, myself, bowed low in the immensity of my sorrow. And so the days pass, the long grey nights ...

67

Newfoundland

Afternoon sunlight slides through the front door as I open it to reach into the mailbox. Oh, an envelope from my publisher, Dundurn Press! I suppose it will be a handful of dollars, if any. Surprise — it's a cheque for $71 for the sales of my first non-fiction book published eighteen year ago. (I get ten percent of the sale price.) I wonder who is still reading about the Canadian Coast Guard after all this time when my material must surely be out of date. That part of my life you didn't know, Gordon. I remember back in 2005 that I invited you to the launch of my second book about heroes published that year and felt disappointed you couldn't come. In my memory, I travel back to that time, to my other life before you: the Canadian Coast Guard and personnel; heroes of all kinds, not only those involving physical danger; writing and publishing books.

I wanted to take you into that life, invite you into what was an all-absorbing few years, so I know what to say when next we ask each other, "Where will we go now?"

"Newfoundland," I reply at once, explaining that a few years ago I drove over all the maritime provinces but not Newfoundland to gather research about the Coast Guard and rescue technicians so I could write about heroism in all its forms. You, like many people, ask me what motivated me, because it seems unlikely that I would do this.

"Let's go to Newfoundland," I say again. "I'll introduce you to my friend, Dave Griffiths, and then you'll know why I did all of this."

Dave, a Coast Guard search-and-rescue (SAR) worker from

Newfoundland, has long befriended me and generously invites us to visit, or did we invite ourselves? Without him, I wouldn't have had access to the Coast Guard hierarchy and had fewer true rescue stories. Next, we're in O'Reilly's Irish pub in St. John's, seated across from Dave and two other SAR techs.

"You'll love all this stuff," I whisper. "Coast Guard rescuers and SAR techs are truly among the most extraordinary people you'll ever meet."

"Except for you," you say, and look at me with that melting expression in your eyes that I love so much. Your elbows are on the table, your eyes alight as you absorb near-mortal tales about daunting rescues, of parachuting to plane crash sites in an Arctic winter.

Our conversations turn to the moral dilemmas that rescuers face, about the sacrificing of the one to save the many. Or the sacrificing of one of their own to save another, often a foolhardy adventurer. The next minute, we're onto psychiatry and laughing about the new definitions of mental illness just added to the *Diagnostic and Statistical Manual of Mental Disorders*.

"How do you know all these things?" I ask, and they explain that they take university courses in their spare time.

"They do these life-and-death things," I say to you afterward, "then run off to university!"

We're invited to Gander to climb over some of the copters, and I watch how much you enjoy all this, remembering also that your father took you and Murray flying and that both of you eventually gained licences.

I should explain that SAR technicians are pararescue specialists trained to perform advanced trauma life support. Their specialties are in military freefall, diving, mountaineering, rappelling, wilderness survival, hoist rescue operations, and various other related tasks. Most of these duties are performed in extreme conditions. They undergo eleven months of initial training at the Canadian Forces School of Search and Rescue based at 19 Wing Comox in British Columbia. Long ago, I understood that the general public knew little about them, and that was my motivation to write three books of true stories about them and to give them recognition.

At Gander, we climb in and out of a stationary Cormorant helicopter and a fixed-wing search-and-rescue aircraft. Again, this is a highlight for you.

We linger in this unique province and decide on a drive down the Avalon Peninsula where, in a ramshackle restaurant, the woman serving us tells us she's from the most northwesterly tip of Vancouver Island's west coast. Indeed, from coast-to-coast. A final drive takes us to the town of Dildo to visit the one-hundred-and-four-year-old grandmother of a neighbour in Toronto — this you particularly want to do for our neighbour, Tyrone. Apparently, Dildo held a plebiscite about changing its name. The town voted no.

. . .

I drag myself from memories of our Newfoundland travel and stare at each featureless day unfolding, the long nights where half awake, half asleep, I think I can hear and feel you beside me. Sometimes you come to me so powerfully that *I* becomes *We*, and there you are, sharing my views, my values, and I all but hear myself say, "Oh, we think this" or "Maybe we can come. We'll let you know." And it's "our house."

One day, I walk home from a meeting at the Exchange Towers, and taking the route through St. James' Park, I imagine living in one of the newish condos built about five, ten, years ago on the northeast corner of Jarvis and Adelaide Streets. It's then that I feel sick at the thought of moving anywhere without you. I walk to the printer on Adelaide, where you used to go, to ask Mohammed if he'll print up more bookmarks that the funeral home gave me, your obituary on one side, Robert Frost's "Carpe Diem" on the other. I plan to send them out with photos, plus a poem of my own, to remember you when six months have been reached. Mohammed remembers you, and his eyes light up at the mention of you. He tells me I need to get the original file. Again, I feel heartsore at going to those places where you've been, to remember that you were here, you were there, now you're nowhere.

. . .

What now? I fly to Kelowna with Helen and Jim to spend time with Paul, Anita, and Lindsay in Interior British Columbia. Many times, you and I, Gordon, made this trip to enjoy our family, which was yours then as much as mine, particularly Lindsay who was born after we got together. How often did we take over their downstairs, sleep in that big bedroom? But what heartache to enter it now, to sense you on your side of the bed, see your silhouette hanging your clothes in the wardrobe, your computer bag leaning against a wall (I'm using it now in memory of you, the same one you always used to carry your laptop in.)

My birthday dawns. On a day streaming with sunshine, Paul, Anita, and I meet at a hilltop winery restaurant for lunch. My son and his wife, having seen me wearing your wedding ring around my neck — but the chain is clumsy — give me a delicate gold-silver chain to wear in its stead. Anita produces a framed poem adapted from something the Swiss-American psychiatrist Elisabeth Kübler-Ross wrote. It reads:

> The Most Beautiful People
> Are those who have known defeat,
> Known loss, and have found
> Their way out of the depths.
> These persons have an
> Appreciation, a sensitivity,
> And an understanding of life
> That fills them with compassion,
> Gentleness, and a deep loving
> Concern. Beautiful people
> Do not just happen.

I weep when I read it. And again, when Helen and Jim present me with a silver locket with a tiny photo of the two of us inserted inside. How lovely. How perfect. I retreat to my bedroom to summon images of you, to remember how you looked at me with your weighted gaze, your particular little smile just for me. I think about the vision you had of me: it was an intoxicating one.

• • •

I'm home again in Toronto after a bittersweet visit. My son, my daughter, and both their families all loved and admired you, Gordon, and once again I feel diminished because I'm only me.

I must tell you about Paul and Anita's cat, Buster, whom we looked after for about four years. He loved you most and missed you terribly. I'm not enough. I'm not you. Realizing the depths of the cat's loneliness, I know that one day I'll return him to them. And November sees me travelling back to the Lake Country with Buster on board. What a trip! I think I'm taking them a dead cat, since about halfway there he heaves in a giant spasm three times, then lies limp for the remainder of the journey.

As I leave, I suddenly realize I need to arrange a visit up north to Cobalt to scatter your ashes, since six months is approaching. This small town of all places in the world is where you'll wish to have your ashes remain.

68

Cobalt: Ashes to Ashes ...

Cobalt, the birthplace of your father, Murray, a small Ontario town, nineteen degrees south of the Arctic Circle. Its streets twist and turn as they run through the town, laid down according to no plan other than to gain easy access to the mineral resources there, particularly huge silver deposits. Across the lake are barren, rocky hills swept clean over a hundred years ago to expose the silver sitting just below the trees and moss. When entering the town from the north or south, towering headframes of remaining mine shafts punctuate the landscape — sentinels to Cobalt's mining heritage. This little town is now identified as one of the most historic areas of Ontario.

Your family's beautiful Gillies house and property lie close to the Montreal River outside Cobalt. Known simply as the Gillies Place and approached by Gillies Depot Road, it has eleven acres of trees, bush, and smooth green lawns. Crowning it is a white villa-style house with green shutters and a partial wraparound verandah close to the river. This house, this property, and the river behind it resonate deeply in the hearts and minds of all the Watts family across many generations. Your parents owned this property, and you, your siblings, your cousins, and the children of all of you loved and idealized it. Long has it become a sacred place, hallowed in memory and living collectively in the dreams of all of you.

I've learned how your many cousins, and in turn your son, Matt, and his cousins roamed its spaces, the surrounding bush, canoed and swam in this part of the Montreal River. Wandered the twisting streets of the little town, haunted the giant bookstore on the highway, and the streets of the neighbouring towns of Haileybury and New Liskeard. It's here we come to scatter your ashes. With the help of the family, I extend invitations to members far and wide. October 6 is the date chosen when we'll all arrive.

Your brother, Murray, drives from Colorado, while his sons fly here. Robert flies from Calgary. Muriel, or Mimi as she's known, and husband, John, come from Guelph. David and his adult children, Jean-Yves, Paloma, and Anik, and David's wife, Tanya, all trek up from Toronto, likewise third sibling, Mary, and Peter Lepic. Matt also comes from Toronto, as well as your nephew, Sean. Cousin Barb flies from Kelowna, Betty and Ken Kramp drive from Barrie, my daughter, Helen, and husband, Jim, from Toronto.

The world, as we drive, is aflame with fall colours at their finest, colours to put a bright face on approaching death, as it's said. The sky arches above, scrubbed clean, then painted the softest blue.

Those four bittersweet days are filled with grief, but also joy in reunion, in shared memories of you, Gordon, and a wonderful sense of family togetherness. About twenty-two of us gather in the Presidential Suites to remember you, to scatter your ashes over that old Gillies property. We give you back to the place you loved: this house, this property with its smooth green lawns, the Montreal River, the town of Cobalt, and even the highway bookshop, of course!

We scatter your ashes as a symbolic release of your soul, and a final goodbye.

Oh, but I'm not ready to say goodbye! And I can't see a time when I ever will.

After strolling the wide-open, beautiful grounds, we meet on the verandah. I quote from Edna St. Vincent Millay's "Dirge Without Music," adapting them into prose:

> Your answers were quick and keen, that honest look, your humour, your love — they are gone. Gone to feed the roses. Elegant and curled is the blossom. Fragrant is the blossom. I know. But I do not approve. More precious was the light in your eyes than all the roses in the world.

Roses. A birthday card smothered in red roses: *I love you more than all the roses in the universe.*

Roses in our garden. Wild roses on the highway, and now roses of all the summers past. But back to the ceremony and the scattering of your ashes, I quote the remainder of Millay's poem:

> Down, down, down into the darkness of the grave
> Gently they go, the beautiful, the tender, the kind;
> Quietly they go, the intelligent, the witty, the brave.
> I know. But I do not approve. And I am not resigned.

No, I am not resigned! I've believed in love. In love at first and last sight. In love everlasting. I found it, and lost it. I lost you. I can never be resigned to this.

Mary says a few words, and Matt a complicated mix of love and angst.

I've brought up boxes of red rose petals to scoop up your ashes that we scatter all about the lawns, among the flowers, on the banks of the Montreal River, and in it.

After more words are said in honour of you, we take boat rides on the river in the canoes David brought up from North Bay.

We return to the Presidential Suites, and I think that if there's a richer, more amiable, warm-hearted group of related people anywhere, I'd like to meet them. We all contribute to and prepare food for meals in the massive kitchen and serve it in the even larger dining and living rooms, a feast three times a day for three days. Conversation hums, laughter and bantering, but with sadness draped over it all.

My beloved, what would you say about yourself, about your life? In the quiet of the northern night, I ask you this and imagine your answer: "I was here. I lived. I loved and was loved. I travelled, walked, and read. I learned and understood. I was a man contented with what was and what is."

I would add this: "And you, so egoless, so modest, could truly have said that you left the mining industry a legacy, that you made life easier and better for your colleagues and for those who succeeded you." Bob Kuehnbaum's words come back to me: "Gord's unique financial schemes were nothing short of brilliant."

Sunday morning dawns as the day before, the blue of the lake mirroring the blue of the arc of the sky. We collect ourselves and tour parts of Cobalt where Mary and Barb once lived, wander about the picturesque railway station, the memorials on the main street, the old shaft building and the once-thriving theatre, and not least, a bookshop.

Sunday afternoon we drop into the ancient Miners' Tavern on the main street where you and I were before, where you and I and Matt lingered.

There, I play table tennis with anyone willing to take me on. Younger people play billiards. How you would love to be with us — well, you are in all our minds.

It's a fitting farewell for you, my darling, but a sad six-hour drive home afterward. I'm keeping the magnificent urn with the remainder of your ashes on the cabinet your mother once owned that you brought into our home. Beside it sits a large photo of you, a vase of red roses, and smaller photos of us grouped around the vase.

Now to the rest of my life and what to do with it — without you.

I know of others who have lost a loved one who managed their grief in various ways, including the friend who immediately gave away her husband's clothes, and within the first month after his death, replaced most of her condo's furniture.

"The sight of it makes me sad," she explained.

"I sat in the house and stared at the walls for two or three years," another said after his wife died.

I, having an irrepressible urge for social activity and a social life, but also seeking distraction, return almost at once to my former activities: to one book club and another, to a writers' group and another. I accept all invitations to dinner and concerts with friends. I join others for coffee, for lunches. But tears are in the back of my eyes and ready to run down my face throughout. Each time I come home to a silent, darkened house at the end of an evening, I creep up to the third floor to commune with you, then return downstairs to the matrimonial bed to pick up my sheaves of photos of you. I fix each one with a penetrating stare as though to do so will bring you back to life. I look and feel the weight of your gaze on me, feel you lurking close by — but where? — then comes a calm, quiet presence to momentarily soften the pain.

Vivid in my memory is that time near the end of August when I feel particularly destitute. It's after my return from the Lake Country in British Columbia with Paul and Anita, and I don't know quite what to do with myself. But I'm saved by my daughter, Helen.

"We're going to the Ex," she says matter-of-factly, talking about the Canadian National Exhibition. "Meet me at one o'clock at the corner of Dundas Street where the streetcars turn."

It's a directive. The day happens to be the very last for the Ex and traditionally is very crowded, rowdy, vibrant.

I obey. Surprise: the day saves me! Among the many hundreds of thousands, we stroll the midway, fascinated, awed even, by the sheer energy and excitement of the masses enjoying sights, rides, entertainment, and an infinite variety of food. Momentary joy courses through me at being among ordinary people doing both ordinary and spectacular things.

One particular early fall day, I walk up Berkeley Street to Carlton Street to do some shopping. A pale sun beams on a late-blooming summer phlox. I notice it, detect the aroma in the air, and feel a faint tinge of pleasure. Immediately, I'm hit by a sense that I'm being disloyal to your memory. How can I enjoy something however small and you are dead? Except for this momentary pleasure, my thoughts are filled with you, and ceaselessly I think of you. I revisit every available memory of you all the while searching for others.

69
One of a Kind

Sometimes I walk downtown to Church and Wellington Streets to visit Dvora Levinson, who lives in the building on that corner. This area of the city both resonates and pains me because so much of your life was lived here: an office on Front Street West, a condo in Market Square, shopping at the St. Lawrence Farmers' Market. I feel you here, feel you inhabiting that lovely area of Toronto. Not least, we, as lovers, met to have drinks in the Down Under Pub in the basement of the Flatiron Building when we were courting. Whenever I walk home from what I consider the heart of Toronto — Front Street, King Street, St. James Cathedral, St. James' Park — I sense you everywhere. It doesn't comfort me, rather, hollowness gathers within me and many times I weep on the way home. But still I like to summon images of you traversing those downtown streets, see your loping stride, how you hold yourself in a particular stance as you move.

After one such visit, strangely, I have an unhappy dream about you, one with portent of the future. You've come from a visit to your doctor and ask me to return with you the next day. Something feels ominous, but I'm happy you want me with you. The dream content fades, but with no resolution. Another dream follows upon this one. I can't recall what it's about, but I wake up crying.

I do weep for you still, but perhaps not as wrenchingly. It's when I realize you're not as sharp and as insistent in my thoughts, my images not as keen, that I fear I'm forgetting you. But then in the most unlikely of places and times, I'll smell the fading perfume of a flower, see the ghastly beauty of a full moon, stars pasted on an evening sky, and my images of you return, sharp and vivid. I hear your voice, feel your presence about me and beside me.

Robes of sound. The hot breath of the sun. I'm back to Virginia Woolf and her image of death's enormous sickle sweeping those tremendous hills, of the lover resting her hoary and immensely aged head at last on the earth … "when the pageant of the universe will be over." At some moments, it feels as though it's over for me, too, having lost you, lost the person I loved with my heart, my body, my soul. But I have a strong impulse to live and perhaps will one day embrace life. Perhaps it will even bloom for me again, together with what you described as my tremendous enthusiasm. But I can't see it, not yet. And the bloom will be pale, dimmed beside what has gone before. How long will it take? I suppose I'm getting used to being alone, of being without you, but there's nothing redeeming about it — nothing!

Someone said to me about you:

You're not lost …
our dearest love …
nor have you travelled far …
you've just stepped outside …
and left the door ajar.

Some images I linger over as solace, sometimes amusement. Girls' Night Out is one. You're not supposed to be there — girls only — but you can't help yourself and come down the stairs to join us, anyway. Afterward, you and I talk and laugh about everyone and everything. How I miss this!

Wendy's birthday party at Kathleen Metcalfe's home on Inglewood Drive is another. You drop me off and say you'll be back to pick me up.

"Come early and you'll get to see it all," I suggest.

You do. I glimpse you hovering in the doorway, that small smile suggesting that, always curious, you know you'll enjoy yourself. And how you do! I feel lit up at the sight of you and proudly announce, "This is my husband."

Yes, this is my husband.

• • •

I turn to guests in the back garden this early fall day. You're at the patio table, with us, and a familiar feeling comes back to me that we're on the same page, the same wavelength. To my joy, you stay. I feel your presence, that you really are here enjoying the conversation. I can tell by the little smile you offer me. Russell says you always surprised people by offering new and original ideas from those expressed. You were truly an intellectual but didn't present yourself as one. These comments call to mind what your colleague, Bob Kuehnbaum, said of you: "Gord was one of a kind. When we got together, our conversations would follow unpredictable, meandering paths through subjects that interested us. Gord often led the way with opinions about all kinds of unusual things and substantiated them with more than a passing understanding. His breadth of knowledge was formidable."

He told me it was his great fortune to have had you as a friend and colleague. Yes! Thank you, Bob!

70

Six Months Is an Eternity

The week of November 11 I feel unwell but disregard the sensation and pull myself out to meet a friend for coffee. As I walk the streets of Cabbagetown in the late afternoon, shadows move across the sidewalks; when opening the door to the house, splintering silence hits me. I stand at the foot of the stairs and call out, "Gordon, where are you? Why don't you come home. You've been away so long!" My sadness is bottomless.

This month, too, is the sixth since you died. I'm driven to commemorate it. Unable physically to hold a memorial for all those who have best known you, I make a plan to post a bookmark with your obituary on one side, Robert Frost's poem "Carpe Diem" on the other. At the bottom, I'll have quotes typed in: "The best portion of a man's life are his little, unremembered acts of kindness and of love." That was you, dear Gordon! I slip a photo of the two of us inside a booklet that has those words in it, as well as other words remembering you. I mail them all over the world to everyone I can recall who has ever known you. In this way, I feel I've celebrated your life — your *gloriosa vita* — and marked its passing.

Drab November stumbles to its close. I lived here with you, Gordon, in this house just the way together we made it. In those ten, eleven years, I felt hugely alive, was young, old, then young again. A ribbon of our life together unspools before me, and I watch how we lived it in Technicolor, intense, vivid. Suddenly, I see a silhouette of myself walking the *corridors of restlessness*, through our living room vivid with paintings and Persian rugs, now climbing the stairs and down again. I love every room, love everything in each of them. As always, and often when I least expect it, your absence hits me and then I feel cold fingers wrap around my heart.

As F. Scott Fitzgerald's last line in *The Great Gatsby* goes: "And so beat on, boats against the current, borne back ceaselessly into the past."

71

Marriage

I'm in the sunroom in front of a blank television, thinking about marriage — this, after time spent in the company of a long-married couple who bicker constantly. It's then I marvel at ours and smile at the memory of how periodically I pinch myself — metaphorically, of course — wondering if ours was real. Truly, the greatest triumph of my life was to have married you!

I think of all the old, tired, never-functioning marriages that lurch through the decades finally to disintegrate. Comments about marriage made by George Eliot in *Middlemarch* come to me:

> [The] smallest sample of virtue or accomplishment is taken to guarantee delightful stores which the broad leisure of marriage will reveal.... Having once embarked on your marital voyage, it is impossible not to be aware that you make no [head]way and

the sea is not within sight — that, in fact, you are exploring an enclosed basin.

Well! In my experience, it's the exact opposite: the "broad pleasures" of our marriage grew broader over the days, the months and the years we spent together. We explored not enclosed basins but a wide-open sea.

My friend, Sarah, comes to dinner. We sit in front of a wood fire eating roast pork and talking about you, about how we met and how we got together. It's Sarah's idea that I write a book for you and suggests the title — *Looking for Gordon* — because she knows Matt and I are always searching for clues to your personality, trying to figure out more fully who you were. "An enigmatic man," your friend and colleague, Charles Pitcher, once said.

One evening, Graeme, always an invaluable source of help and strength, joins me for dinner. Matt visits the next day. When Matt and I are together, we talk about you, each of us adding to the other's store of knowledge. The day after, I drive out to Oakville to attend Helen's book-and-knitting club. You'd laugh at the idea that I might take up knitting and won't be surprised to learn that as yet I haven't. I enjoy this group, first, because I love books and literature, second, because it's a different age group and people are engaged in occupations other than those I'm familiar with, and so I get new ideas and perspectives.

72

More Images

It's December. I've made it all the way here! One morning, I awake, and in a strange mood decide to clean up the house, the basement, and in a frenzy, rush downstairs to begin — oh, but where to start? You were a hoarder, a collector. I commence by scrubbing and painting the basement tiles, by sorting stuff and cleaning shelves. There must be some psychological interpretation of this drive to do this, to get rid of stuff. I carry a collection of fans, leather bags, and small lamps out onto the sidewalk where they quickly disappear.

My mission to sort and clean up the basement continues for some time. It's always bothered me that it's such a mess, even if it's only used for laundry and storage — and the cat litter box. My next mission is to organize my clothes in the walk-in closet. I need a place to store sheets and towels, since I'm about to rent the back bedroom and bathroom two nights a week and have been using the chest of drawers there as a linen closet. I remove your sweaters from a shelf in the closet and place the sheets there. The next time I open that door I see the sheets in place of your sweaters and am completely undone. Immediately, I return your sweaters to the shelf.

After my cleaning binge subsides, I climb the stairs to the third floor, sit in your empty chair, and summon you to me. I'm still looking for you, Gordon. But my images are, as once before, blurred, diminished. Your pair of running shoes seem emptied out, like a colour photo that's faded. Your collection of rocks and crystals, your eye charts on the wall — all are beginning to disappear into the background.

"Where are you?" I cry out, and try to call you back, will myself to see your blue eyes gazing at me with that familiar smile inside them.

One evening, I go downstairs to make some sort of dinner for myself. I call out to you that it's ready, then wait to hear your footsteps on the stairs. Catching sight of you in the many photos around the kitchen, I tell myself:

I've been lucky.

I've been happy.

Happy? Did I know that at the time?

Again, I recall someone saying happiness is only a memory. Really? Others declare it to be the path itself.

A flicker of joy ripples through me as I study your face in the photos, as I recall the many times I trimmed your eyebrows, smoothed the shaggy look of you in the mornings, rumpled your hair and adjusted your shirt collar. Images flit of you disappearing down the street with your particular unhurried rhythm, sloping along the corridor downstairs, stretching your tall, lean form on the living room couch, emerging through the doorway into the bedroom. But every time I glimpse you, you fade from sight. Sightings of you suggest who you are and what you think and feel, your appearance inclining others to trust who you are. And to think that you were mine!

73

Christmas

Christmas — I've always loved it, but this year I dread it. Maintaining ceremonial and traditional events is so rooted in me, however, that I resolve to have decorations put up, which David does for me.

One night, I look out our bedroom window that faces the street to see a lopsided moon caught in the branches of the big chestnut tree, to spot neighbours Greg Adair and Louis-Phillipe busy preparing to hold a best house Christmas decorations contest. For this, neighbours are invited to gather, eat, drink, and cast a vote. That appointed evening, each of us is handed a glass of mulled wine. Then we gather in Greg's house to be treated to a feast of elaborate proportions catered by both men, are offered more wine, and finally asked to vote.

The votes are counted by a lawyer, so of course it's a tie! I'm reminded of another evening hosted by Louis-Phillipe: a barbecue in the backyard, and in the soft night air, a neighbour raising his voice and singing "A Nightingale Sang in Berkeley Square." Ah, yes, Berkeley Street.

Two Christmas dinners this year, one with the Watts family, the other with the Taylor family at Graeme's condo. I manage it with smiles during the day but weeping in the night.

Then comes a dreaded New Year's Eve. At the home of Di Thomson and Barry Little following a Beethoven concert, everything goes well until the singing of "Auld Lang Syne" on a local television station: "Lest old acquaintance be forgot … and never brought to mind …" The words and the singing break my heart. When it's repeated at the stroke of midnight, I rush to the bathroom and turn on the fan to block out the sounds.

How dreary is the first morning of a new year and the thought of all the empty days and years to follow. I ache for our old sense of belonging, for that profound intimacy, the two of us in synergy with, or against, the world. I summon you to my side when I invite myself to have lunch with your colleague and friend, Lee Barker, when I ask him about you, since he knew you since university and shared a flat with you. Still looking for you, Gordon!

"What was Gordon like in his university years and all the years after?" I ask him.

"Quiet" comes the laconic answer. "Always unhurried. He didn't participate much in social situations, but when a subject interested him, he would talk freely about it. I asked his opinions about many things and knew he would have answers. He did. He had an extraordinary amount of knowledge."

He pauses, then says, "After he met you, he loosened up a lot. He smiled and laughed a lot more."

Thank you for this, Lee!

"He was also a guy who could do a lot of things," Lee adds.

I know. And I remember that you:

Fly an aircraft.

Sail a boat.

Ride a bicycle, skate, rollerblade, ski. Walk.

Love me. Marry me!

I ask you, "Gordon, what do you think? What should I do? How should I be?"

I tell you I love you. I just love you so much!

74

Brothers

I enjoy January and its full blast of winter, but because no winter sport is possible for me anymore, I arrange social get-togethers. As I do, I remember Virginia Woolf's Mrs Dalloway and her parties, how her old friend, Peter Walsh, asks why she gives them. "They are my offering," she tells him.

They are my offering, too, and I do them now for my very sanity.

One such get-together is with the Watts family. We decide to hold these on a regular basis because we're all spooked at how easily and swiftly a person's life is snuffed out, how fragile it all is, this thing called life. Then there's the whole idea of family. You were your family's go-to person, Gordon, the glue that seemed to hold everything together.

The strong kinship among the Watts brothers once prompted me to write about a memorable occasion, rare in your adult lives because of the geographic distances that separate you. First comes Murray from Colorado, not seen in Toronto in many years. You swoop upon him, Gordon — well, not swoop, since that's not what you do. But I see your little smile, one that could light up a dungeon. You're joined by Robert from Calgary sometime later, three brothers seeking to rekindle a brotherly past.

As you talk into the night, I realize you're on a mission I don't understand, one you haven't articulated even to yourselves. Your talk becomes like rapid-fire pellets flying about and hanging in the air, swallowed up before being digested. Then comes another round, and another, words fired into the split-second space when one mouth closes and another opens.

Words race around the kitchen, up to the ceilings, and fasten themselves on walls and on the floor: Goldman Sachs. Crooks. Felons. Greed as a sickness, the whole world mortgaged. IOUs issued instead of salaries. California dead broke and the feds not interested. Who will pay? No one can pay. It's all like a house of cards: a global collapse and no future. The Chinese. Copper. Ah, yes, that's the thing. Copper? Are you serious?

The small hours of the night — or should it be called the morning? — sidle upon us. The words do not slow but change. The present slips away, and with it the whole world's mess.

The hands on the clock fall backward. Three men become little boys again:

You did that?

No, I never did.

Remember the time when ... Mom, was she ever mad! But you were so funny ... I never told, I swear, but you got me in trouble. Hey, was it you who put a mouse inside the grandfather clock? And I never did put it in your bed afterward — truly!

The art deco clock chimes five. I walk to the window and see that it's stopped raining, become aware that the flow of words has ceased. In the near-perfect silence that follows, the brothers begin laughing, flinging arms around one another as each emerges from a time capsule — your shared childhood viewed now as a perfect and unparalleled time that can be visited at will.

75

I Will Meet You at the Empty Door

February, the bitterest of winter months: I join the Arts & Letters Club on Elm Street, something not fraught for me since you were never part of it and never entered its premises. I force myself to do these things: to write, to edit, to attend a writers' group, a book club. I drive out to Oakville to my daughter's book club.

It's when I come home from anywhere and walk through that empty door — *I will meet you at the empty door* — that the silence in the house mocks me, its walls echoing as I climb the stairs to sit in your empty chair. I look about at all you've abandoned and cry out, "Where are you?"

Next, neighbour Greg calls and asks me to dinner.

Shopping. I do it for us. I come home. *What did you get for me?* So many ghosts!

Tuesday night is the Arts & Letters Club Writers' Circle Meeting. I walk there. I say and do the appropriate things. I walk home.

On Wednesday, Matt and Rick come to dinner. I enjoy memories of the evening as I write this, recalling how you always said, "That went well," after events you enjoyed, which were most things.

Right now, if you're anywhere near watching me, you'll see that I push on and do most of the things I've always done. But come a little closer, feel the river of sadness that runs through me, how it's exacerbated by little things such as making the bed — of all things! It's because we made it together. Something more and big: I was my very best self when I was with you.

76
Ellicottville

A new country — well, a different one — and a sea change for me: the company of my beloved daughter, Helen, for a few days in Ellicottville, Upstate New York. Only this: that it's here where you and I spent days and long weekends together, in this house, in this pretty little town's coffee bars and restaurants, in the arboretum close by. As with my sojourn in British Columbia's Lake Country with my beloved son and family, I feel a return of that heartache I've learned to become afraid of, a blunt force hitting me, of cold stones sliding through me. I hear us laughing on the tennis courts, see us leaning over each other across a Scrabble board. Instinctively, I look for you in the blue bedroom. I reach out for you. My hands are empty.

Home again, and a day when I feel good enough to get on the elliptical machine and do thirty minutes, to go shopping, go to the bank. But as always when I've returned home from somewhere, anywhere, I step into a house echoing with emptiness, silent as a fox on ice. It's then that I feel defeated. Before, when things went wrong, even horribly wrong, I worked to make it all better and so right the disequilibrium. I did anything and everything, twisted my thoughts and emotions into a place where I felt things might be okay and some sort of normalcy restored.

None of that works anymore.

77

Mexico

In March 2020, your sister, Mary, and I leave for ten days in San Miguel de Allende, Mexico. We stay in an Airbnb high on a slope above the city. You and I, Gordon, often talked about visiting this little place in the mountains, renowned for its art, music, museums, and galleries. I'm happy being somewhere else and being with Mary, who is a little bit of you, but entering my room hits me hard: its outsize bed, its huge space, the emptiness of it. The solitariness of it forces me out, and I go up on the rooftop alone.

For northerners, Mexico means warmth and sunshine. It's not warm here — not yet. Scattered sunlight sifts through shifting clouds, but the air is clear and the view is both near and distant. I summon you, my darling. I need to feel your presence, to talk to you, to share my thoughts. Is it your ghost I feel, or are you really here? You smile at everything the way you do when you're contented, which is most of the time. Immediately upon this comes a now-familiar sense of loss, and I think all over again: *How can I do this?*

As the days pass, I wander in desultory fashion with Mary to see the town, its cathedrals, art, novelty shops, and marketplaces. We take a bus ride to an adjacent city and wander around it. Mary tours the city's architectural gems with a group of others. I remain in my room, my laptop open, writing to you.

One afternoon, we sign up for a few hours' bus tour of the town. At the peak of a hill, we get off and are given fifteen minutes before boarding and continuing. When we turn around, the bus and all the people have gone! Mary is furious. She tries unsuccessfully to get us a refund. My usual enthusiasm when in new surroundings refuses to appear, and I wonder if that part of my life and who I was is over forever.

When we were at David's before our trip to Mexico, Mary told us she lost fifteen pounds in weight since you died, Gordon. She weeps for you and says the family has become fractured since your death, all of us drifting apart.

"Matt has changed, everyone has changed," she said.

"No, it's we who have changed," I told her.

It's a new world that emerges not long after Mary and I return from Mexico. History will use various labels to refer to it, but the new coronavirus is generally referred to simply as COVID-19, or the Time of COVID. It means we're all locked inside our homes in strict isolation. At first, for two weeks, then extended repeatedly for another two weeks and another and another.

A year and more have passed since you died. *A year.* In Maggie O'Farrell's novel *Hamnet*, the husband, William Shakespeare, says to his wife, Anne Hathaway, at the death of their eleven-year-old son, Hamnet, "It's been a year."

"A year is nothing," she replies with emphasis.

78

A Year Is Nothing

A year is nothing. One year since you died, and still I look for you. As Maggie O'Farrell says of Hamnet's mother, "I'm constantly wondering where he [Hamnet] is, where has he gone." Whatever I'm doing, wherever I am, I, too, think, where are you? You can't have just vanished. You must be somewhere. All I have to do is find you, and I keep searching for you in every street, in every crowd ... trying to find a version of you.

Anne Hathaway in *Hamnet* says, "We may never stop looking for him [Hamnet]." I don't think I'll ever want to stop looking for you.

Wishing to mark one year since your death, to have you remembered, and to celebrate your life, I banish the whistling emptiness inside me and think about what I can do. Because of COVID-19 and the stay-at-home orders, no one can gather anywhere, with anyone. It's then that I send out another communication, this time only by email, in which I quote excerpts from the Reverend Rick Fee, and my own comments as below:

IN MEMORY OF GORDON WATTS WHO LEFT US ON MAY 21, 2019

It is a beautiful world because Gordon was here, and so much remains of what he contributed to make it beautiful. In this intelligent, humble, easygoing "Uncle Tree" we saw a man who was a problem-solver, a man who had no ego, who loved his solitary life and was happy in his own company. He shared love, was fulfilled in his relationship with Carolyn, and garnered respect from his colleagues around the world …

While his physical presence has been removed, his professional accomplishments, his encouraging words, his warm nature, are not forgotten. What remains is the good that he did, the lessons he shared, the time he took to instruct. These are his legacy. We bid farewell to such a soul as we have been privileged to know, that now and forever, the day breaks, and the shadows flee away.

From me to you, Gordon (adapted from Virginia Woolf's *Mrs Dalloway*:

You came to me swiftly out of the night, a lone figure on silent feet, and just as swiftly, you were gone. Now I wander through nights and days to dwell alone among my memories. I loved you with all my heart and my soul, my love to last a million years. And millions of years ago, you who had been with me these centuries, had walked. And in the course of ages, long as summer days, and flaming, I remembered that you had gone.

On the exact anniversary of your death, Gordon, I invite Mary and Matt to dine, to raise a glass or two to you, to remember you. We're not allowed to have more than two or three people together right now, and David and Tanya have disappeared up north for about six months.

• • •

It's June, and I'm getting ready for Francine to come over. I feel you in the house today, darling, and am comforted. It's not a sensation that comes often, because one minute you're here with me, the next you're not. Then cold loneliness hits me. *Where are you?*

I walk through our house often, admiring what we put together: three-hundred-year-old church doors shipped from Cairo to greet you as you enter. Deep brown walls in the dining room and a stained-glass window retrieved from an old church. The living room: cream-coloured leather couches and walls covered with oil-based and watercolour paintings, many of them Turkish and Greek. And the dining room table: it belonged to my parents, built for them from scarce New Zealand oak. I had it shipped to Singapore, up to British Columbia, and trucked across Canada. It's an object of beauty, and when I look at it, I try to banish images of slain forests. Then the sunroom: we lived in it, lived as though we were outdoors.

It's all mine now. I feel the joy, the burden …

You come to me sometimes, like the spirit of a newborn day visiting the dark vault where I sit, the bride of a thinned-out life. I interpret that you spent very little of your heart before me, and I look at myself to see what you saw, peer in the mirror, only to see a haunted creature staring at sorrow.

I walk through Allan Gardens beneath the magnificent trees, smelling their perfume and the aromas of flowers. As I walk, I feel pleasure sitting on a stone bench in the sun, stretching my legs and feeling my feet warmed. No longer do I feel quite so acutely that I'm being unfaithful to your memory because of my pleasure in these things. But the pleasure is bittersweet. I want to say, "Look at that twisting trunk, Gordon. Smell the perfumes of the trees!" Always to share my pleasure doubles it. But then I recall the yogi instructor who had a disciple he never allowed to walk with him in the evenings to watch a sunset. Until one day, he relented. As the two strolled along the ridge of a hill, as the sunset glowed pink and orange in its slow descent toward the horizon, the disciple exclaimed in wonder, "Just look! It's so beautiful!"

"I'm sorry, but you cannot walk with me anymore," the yogi master said sadly.

"But why ever not?" The disciple was puzzled and disappointed.

"Because when you point out what you see and admire, you are not truly absorbing its beauty for yourself."

79

What to Do with Love

It's late one evening when I walk upstairs and to bed. Reaching the top step, I pause in the doorway of my office, then look up as always to your darkened, silent third floor. A feeling creeps over me that I've suffered a long illness, that I'm getting better but am still fragile, as though I could easily slip back into the bitter night that has been my year since you died.

June 27, and your birthday. I remember a marriage prayer from the Book of Tobit: "Mercifully, grant that we may grow old together." We were already old when we met, but I hoped, I assumed, we'd have many more years to love and grow older together.

About love: here is Franz Kafka to speak to it.

The renowned Bohemian novelist and short-story writer lived between 1883 and 1924. He never married and had no children. One afternoon, while strolling through Steglitz Park in Berlin, he chanced upon a young girl crying because she lost her favourite doll. She and Kafka searched for the doll without success. Kafka told her to meet him in the same place the next day and they'd look again.

That day, when they still hadn't found the doll, Kafka gave the girl a letter "written" by the doll that said, "Please do not cry. I have gone on a trip to see the world. I'm going to write to you about my adventures."

Thus, began a story that continued to the end of Kafka's life. When they would meet, Kafka read aloud his carefully composed letters of adventures and conversations about the beloved doll, which the girl found enchanting. Finally, Kafka read her a letter of the story that brought the doll back to Berlin. He then gave her a doll he'd purchased.

"This does not look at all like my doll," she said.

Kafka handed her another letter that explained: "My trips, they have changed me." The girl hugged the new doll and took it home with her. A year later, Kafka died. Many years later, the now grown-up girl found a letter tucked into an unnoticed crevice in the doll. The tiny letter, signed by Kafka, said: "Everything you love is very likely to be lost, but in the end, love will return in a different way."

• • •

It's now thirteen, fourteen months since you died, Gordon. I'm in Oakville with my granddaughter, Cameron, while Helen and Jim are away. Cameron is working as a lifeguard, on duty for eleven hours. I shop, walk, write, then stroll in the local cemetery called St. Jude's. Interesting and beautiful trees soar above the headstones, including many species of pines. I can't identify them but admire them. Again, I feel a shaft of pain because you're not there to share this with me, that I can't go home to tell you. More than that, still I feel it desecrates your memory that I'm enjoying this without you.

I live under a pale, wan sun. I still do what I always do. It's a very hot summer, and those who don't have backyards want to come and sit in mine. Once, only once, do I feel I'm being slowly stitched back together, just a tiny bit. While visiting Di and Barry, fleetingly, I think I'm getting to be a little more than half of myself.

But then tonight, in Oakville again walking in the local cemetery, I sit on a bench to rest among the green, the trees, the birdsong. And it returns, that sense of aloneness, of solitariness and myself a half person. I talk to you, tell you that you should be here with me.

How could you have abandoned me? I cry silently as I've done so many times before.

It's July 9, 2020, and I've just returned from grocery shopping at No Frills, and while heading toward home down Berkeley Street, I think about what I've read somewhere about most of us not enjoying the present because we're so immersed in the past, or gazing at an imagined future. I think of all the enjoyment I've been getting with the big blue sun umbrella you ordered long ago but that we never put up, not knowing how to fasten it to the fence or the deck. I've had many people come to sit under it in both sun and rain — so sheltering. I remember you've never seen it.

I see a featureless future stretching before me, punctuated only rarely by the flare of something less gloomy, less dull.

At your death, Gordon, I feel I lost my heart's last outward leap, that the elastic has quite gone.

I think real love is truly a miracle. You wait for it to happen. You wait, and wait some more, and it almost never does happen. If you're lucky enough, you find it. It's a gift from God — whoever or whatever God is.

80

Healing Is Remembering Well

Hello, darling, a note to you. (I still write to you most evenings.) I just spent a week with Charles Pitcher. It was weird being up there in Bobcaygeon without you, but we talked about you, and in some way, you were there. I think of our conversations as I walk in Regent Park, as I sit on a bench and look at the trees. Suddenly, I have an odd feeling that I don't know where I am — well, I do — but sense myself to be without an anchor, that I could be anywhere and who will care? A heavy shroud of sadness drapes over me, and all too quickly tears come to my eyes. *I just really miss you!* I read somewhere that while grief is universal, it's also singular and very personal. There's no time limit on it. The pain now has to be the happiness that was then. Healing isn't forgetting but remembering well.

Even now, after fifteen months, I stroll my familiar evening route down Berkeley Street, and suddenly, to use Cathy's words to Heathcliff in *Wuthering Heights*, it turns into a "mighty stranger." I'm that stranger in a strange land that I've long inhabited. I look at the trees, the parked cars alongside the pretty Victorian houses, curtains drawn against the deepening dusk, and I see it for the first time. Because you're not in it. And I lay my suddenly "immensely aged head" on my pillow and weep. *Where are you? How could you leave me?*

I wander along Dundas Street all the way to Dundas Square, the route we so often took together. It might be to a movie, or to that wonderful coffee house on Yonge Street, or to bookstores. I walk there today more than a year and a half after you died. Memories that come to me of those ordinary events are the sweetest, most precious, that a person can hold. But they come together with a bruised heart.

In Virginia Woolf's *To the Lighthouse*, a reader spends one hundred and twenty-five pages getting to know Mrs Ramsay — the matriarch and centre of the novel — only to lose her in a single sentence: "[Mr Ramsay stumbling along a passage stretched his arms out one dark morning, but, Mrs Ramsay having died rather suddenly the night before, he stretched his arms out. They remained empty.]

The brackets suggest the empty arms of Mr Ramsay; they punctuate death with their embrace. Death enters suddenly and shatters the familial bonds that Woolf has been examining in meticulous detail. Putting Mrs Ramsay's death in brackets and in a subordinate clause seems cruel and ironic, tinged with aggression and the desire to shock, but the absence of detail and explanation makes me think of the arbitrariness and impersonality of death in relation to life. I understand now the deliberateness of this structure, the experience of loss represented on the page. The velocity of your death and my distance from it all feel like a death in brackets. There is no touch, no contact. There are no final conversations, no holding the hand of the dying.

How am I to live? You've finished your journey, but I trudge on. I feel you've floated off to some other, better place, glided from your third-floor office while I climb those steep steps after you. I want to go with you but don't know where that is, and still silently I cry, "Come back!"

Perhaps I should let memories of you come to me as they will throughout the day, rather than summoning them, summoning you, to me, stop looking for you. But how hard it is to move on from our histories, move through days that are shapeless, without colour. How was it that in the vastness of human nature, by some fluke, we found each other?

Someone tells me there will be a time when a smile will come before a tear when I remember you.

How much time?

The beauty of who you are and were has marked my heart forever. I know you're not coming back, know, to quote Dylan Thomas, that "Though lovers be lost love shall not; and death shall have no dominion." I have to go forward, but I'll be carrying you with me in my heart for … the rest of my days.

Lightning Source UK Ltd.
Milton Keynes UK
UKHW020208110122
396920UK00009B/1956